"Do you thin[k] brother's chi[ld]—[my] son—to be born out of wedlock? Such a thing is unthinkable, a dishonor."

"Toni is dead. I can't marry him."

"Of course not," Rinaldo said coldly. "It is necessary that you marry me.... I advise that you give my suggestion serious consideration."

"Was it a suggestion?" Donna asked ironically. "It sounded more of a diktat to me."

"Well, I can't force you, can I? I can only suggest and ask you to consider. Your own life will be comfortable. Why should you refuse?"

"Why?" she echoed, scandalized. "Because you've been my enemy from the first moment. Because there could never be peace between us. Because I dislike you intensely."

Dear Reader,

A special new delivery! We are proud to announce the birth of our new bouncing baby series! Each month we'll be bringing you your very own bundle of joy—a cute and delightful romance by one of your favorite authors. This series is all about the true labor of love—parenthood and how to survive it! Because, as our heroes and heroines are about to discover, two's company and three (or four...or five) is a family!

This month, it's the turn of Lucy Gordon with *His Brother's Child*. Next month's arrival will be (#3453) *First-Time Father* by Emma Richmond.

Happy reading!

The Editors

His Brother's Child
Lucy Gordon

Harlequin Books

TORONTO • NEW YORK • LONDON
AMSTERDAM • PARIS • SYDNEY • HAMBURG
STOCKHOLM • ATHENS • TOKYO • MILAN
MADRID • WARSAW • BUDAPEST • AUCKLAND

ISBN 0-373-03450-4

HIS BROTHER'S CHILD

First North American Publication 1997.

Copyright © 1997 by Lucy Gordon.

CHAPTER ONE

'IS IT much further to Rome?' Donna asked eagerly.

'Another ten miles.' Toni glanced sideways to give her a glowing smile. 'You're beautiful, *carissima*. My family will fall in love with you at first sight—just like I did.'

'Darling, please keep your eyes on the road,' she begged nervously.

He laughed and obeyed. 'All right, madam schoolmistress,' he mocked.

'Don't say that. I don't really sound like a schoolmistress, do I?'

'Of course you do. My delightful, adorable schoolmistress, always telling me off. Toni, drive more slowly. Toni, don't be so extravagant. Toni, don't—'

'Oh, *no*!' she cried, half laughing, half dismayed. 'Now you make me sound like a dragon.'

'But I like it. You're very good for me. My brother Rinaldo will be grateful to you for keeping me in order. It's something he's never managed yet.'

He spoke with his usual cheery good nature, but to Donna it was a reminder that, at twenty-seven, she was three years Toni's senior. That was something she tried not to dwell on, but it was hard when Toni still had so much of the boy in him. She regarded his profile with affection. He had vivid Latin good looks, typical of the south of Italy, where he'd been born. She remembered how her friends had envied her when he'd started to pursue her!

She'd met Toni Mantini in the hospital where she was a nurse, and where he'd been brought after his car had lost an argument with a lamppost. He'd described the accident to her with rueful humour. That was typical of Toni, she'd discovered. To him life was laughter and pleasure. His injuries were slight, the insurance would pay for the car. Why worry?

Just what there was in her serious nature that had attracted this careless Italian boy she'd never been able to work out. But when he was discharged from hospital he'd returned persistently until she'd agreed to go out with him. After that things had moved at a speed that left her breathless.

He told her that he loved her, often and passionately. The knowledge filled her with wonder. Toni was vibrantly handsome. Her own looks, she thought disparagingly, were those of a little brown mouse.

'But no,' he'd said when she'd voiced this thought. 'You look like a Madonna, with your calm oval face, your dark hair and your big eyes. Near my family's home in Rome there's a little church with a picture of the Madonna and child. I'll take you there one day, and you'll see yourself. Never change, *carissima*. You are beautiful just as you are.'

It had never occurred to her that she might be beautiful, and she loved Toni for showing her to herself in that new light. She loved him for so many things— his eagerness for life, his boyish enthusiasm that could make him reckless, his careless laughter. But most of all she loved him because he loved her.

It was early afternoon now, and the Italian sun was high.

'Does the heat bother you?' Toni asked as she mopped her brow.

'It's a bit overwhelming, after England,' she admitted. 'I shall be glad to get into the cool.'

'Poor darling. You can rest this afternoon. Tomorrow we'll go out shopping and I'll buy you some new clothes, and jewels. I'd like to see you in rubies.'

She laughed. 'What a dreamer you are, darling. You know you can't afford rubies, even if I wanted them.'

'Who says I can't?'

'You're behind with the repayments on this car.'

His face was a picture of innocence. 'Behind? Me? Whatever gave you that idea?'

She chuckled. 'I answered the phone to the finance company, remember?'

'Oh, well!' He abandoned the pretence with a shrug. 'Just a little bit behind. Not angry with me, are you, *cara*?'

'How can I be angry with you?' she asked tenderly.

How could she be anything but passionately grateful to this young man who'd brought warmth and colour into her lonely life? He wanted her. That was the glorious, unbelievable fact that flooded the world with light and gave her a happiness she'd never even dreamed of before.

It was so long since she'd been wanted by anyone. When she was seven years old her father had left home for another woman. After the divorce he'd kept in touch with her sporadically, sometimes even taken her out. But he'd never taken her home to meet his new wife and child, and Donna had come to understand, without it actually being said, that there was no place for her in that family.

Then her mother had died. Donna was ten. Now, surely, her father would claim her? And he'd promised to do so 'when things are a little easier'. But it had seemed the time was never right, and at last she'd lost hope completely.

She'd spent the rest of her childhood in care. There had been two foster homes, one of which had broken up in divorce. The other family had simply taken on too many children. Donna was fourteen by then, old enough to help out. She hadn't minded. She'd liked caring for the little ones, and it was good to be needed. But her foster mother had made it clear that she was there to be useful, and it wasn't the same as being wanted for herself.

When she'd left care at sixteen she'd made determined efforts to stay in touch, sending cards at Christmas and on birthdays, and thinking of them as 'my family'. But the cards were never answered. One day, paying a surprise visit, she'd found strangers living there. The family had moved away without telling her.

With such a background it was hardly surprising that she'd found Toni irresistible. Everything about him was enchanting in her eyes, even his nationality. Italy had always been the country of Donna's dreams. She'd planned to take a holiday there, and had even learned the language in readiness. But on a nurse's pay her savings mounted very slowly, so the Italian holiday had been put off, year after year, while she continued to weave her bright dreams. She pictured Italy as a colourful, light-hearted place, full of warm families that clung together. She was sorry Toni's family wasn't larger, only a grandfather and an older brother. But the affectionate way he spoke of them made her eager to meet them.

And now, soon, she would do so. And soon she would no longer be lonely Donna Easton, but Signora Mantini, bearing a Mantini child.

The thought made Donna lay a hand reverently across her stomach. It was much too soon for anything to show, but already the baby was precious to her. It would be hers and Toni's, linking them for ever as part of a true family.

When she'd told him she was pregnant she'd half expected the worst. Surely this careless charmer didn't want to be tied down to a family at twenty-four? But Toni had been overwhelmed with joy, repeating, 'You're going to be a mother...' many times in an awed voice. He'd become even more loving and tender to her, and her love for him had grown.

He'd insisted that they marry 'as soon as you have met my family'. She never knew what was said in his phone call to his brother Rinaldo, but he'd announced that they must go to Italy immediately.

'I've said only that I'm bringing my bride,' he told her. 'We'll tell them about the baby when we get there.'

'I'll get leave of absence from the hospital,' she said.

'No, no! You don't go back there. Give them notice.'

'Toni, I don't think that's wise.'

'My wife does not work!' he announced with a lordly finality that made her lips twitch. He noticed her trying to suppress her laughter, and grinned. 'OK, OK! I get a proper job. Perhaps I go into the business with Rinaldo and we live over there.'

'In Italy?' she said excitedly. 'That would be wonderful.'

'Good. It's settled!'

Toni was like that. Donna could have sworn that five minutes ago he'd had no notion of working in Italy. But suddenly it was settled.

A few days later they'd loaded their things into the car and started the long journey across the Channel,

through France, then Switzerland, and into Italy. They'd
stopped overnight several times, because Toni didn't want
to tire her, and had spent last night in Perugia. This
morning they had started early for the final stretch of
road that would lead to Rome.

'Tell me some more about your family,' she begged
now.

Toni shrugged. 'Nothing much to tell. Rinaldo is all
right, but he's a bit of a bore. Thinks about nothing but
business, as though making money was the only thing
in the world that counted.'

'Well, if you're in business you need to make a
reasonable profit,' Donna said. 'Didn't you say he sends
you an allowance?'

'Oh, if you're going to talk common sense I give up.
All right, the business pays my allowance, but that's no
reason for brooding on it night and day, the way Rinaldo
does.'

'What exactly is the business? You've always been very
vague about it.'

'Engineering. Machine tools. One of the factories
makes medical equipment.'

'Factories? Plural?' Donna frowned. She'd had a
vague impression of the Mantini family as modestly
prosperous. It had never occurred to her that they were
richer than that.

'Six factories,' Toni said. 'No, it's five now. Rinaldo
sold one because it wasn't meeting its performance
targets. He believes in cutting his losses.'

Donna wasn't sure why the suggestion of wealth should
disturb her, but it did. For the first time she had doubts
about her ability to fit in. Then she thrust them aside.
Even the owner of five factories might not live luxur-
iously. He probably ploughed the profits back into the

business and lived modestly. She began to feel more comfortable.

'Didn't you ever want to go into the business yourself?' she asked.

'Heaven forbid! All that dreary grind! Mind you, Rinaldo was always on at me to learn about machines. He'll be glad of you. He wants to see me married. He says it will 'steady' me. Also, he wants an heir to take the business over.'

'Why doesn't he have his own heir?'

'Because it would mean getting married, and Rinaldo's relationships with women are all very short-lived. He prefers it that way. He says no woman can be trusted.'

'But he wants you to do what he won't do himself?'

Toni chuckled good naturedly. 'The way he puts it, I'm bound to make a fool of myself one way or another, so it may as well be the married way. Then at least I'll be doing something useful.'

'He sounds charming—I don't think.'

'Well, he glowers a bit, and he's got a very nasty temper,' Toni admitted. 'It doesn't do to get on his wrong side. But don't worry. I told you, he'll like you.'

To Donna's relief they were coming to the end of the *autostrada*, the long motorway whose uninterrupted vista had tempted Toni to hair-raising feats of speed. There followed a series of turns too complex for her to follow, and then they were driving along a wide, grassy avenue lined with cypress trees.

'This is the Appian Way,' Toni told her. 'A lot of Italian film stars have villas along here.'

'How thrilling! Is it much further to where we're going?'

'No, we're about five villas along.'

'You mean—your family lives on the Appian Way?'

'Of course,' Toni said in a matter-of-fact voice. 'Here we are.'

He swung the car through a wide gate and Donna found herself in grounds that seemed to go on for ever. The road ahead curved in and out of trees and shrubs. Gradually a building came into view. At first sight it seemed a simple house, with yellow walls and a red tiled roof. But as they drew nearer Donna saw how large it was, and how it branched off into wings.

Trees surrounded it and baskets of flowers, filled with geraniums, hung from the balconies. Birds called, and from somewhere Donna could hear the soft plashing of water.

It was all incredibly beautiful, but Donna's pleasure was marred by a growing sense of unease. Only a family of great wealth could own a dwelling such as this, and she felt a shrinking inside her. What was she doing in this luxurious place?

Toni brought the car to a halt outside the big front door. There was no sign of life. The house might have been deserted.

'Let's go in and see who's about,' he said, offering his hand to help her out.

Donna's discomfort increased when they entered the house and she saw the marble floor and sweeping marble staircase. The hallway was like a large room in itself. Doors led off to unseen regions. Between the doors were niches housing small statues surrounded by plants. In the midday heat the hall had an air of spacious coolness.

'I'll go and find someone,' Toni said. 'Wait for me here.'

He vanished down a passage, calling, 'Is anybody at home?' leaving Donna to study her surroundings. She hoped Toni would return quickly, before strangers found her here.

Then she noticed something. To her left a narrow corridor led to an open door, through which she could see daylight. She knew she ought to remain here until Toni came for her, but something seemed to draw her, as though by hypnotism, along the corridor to the light.

She found herself in a courtyard, surrounded by cloisters. Here the gleaming marble floor ended, and there were rough flagstones underfoot. The cloisters were about four feet wide, with the wall of the house on one side and arches supported by decorated pillars on the other. In the courtyard she could see a pool, with a fountain in the centre. Flower baskets hung from the windows above, and white doves cooed and fluttered around a dovecote.

The cloisters took up three sides. The fourth side was a wall, against which a staircase ran to the upper floor. Flowers trailed through the gaps between the supports of the stone balustrade and hung down.

Donna regarded the scene ecstatically. The place had a rustic, weather-beaten charm that spoke of centuries. Lichen grew over the stone. The walls were red, brown, faded yellow. This was the Italy of her dreams.

On one wall a few words had been chiselled into the stone. They said simply, *'Il giardino di Loretta'*.

'Loretta's garden,' Donna murmured to herself. Whoever Loretta had been she'd loved this place with her whole heart. Her love still breathed through every plant, every vista of beauty.

Wherever Donna looked there were flowers—jasmine, clematis, bougainvillea, oleander—filling the air with their heady perfume. Entranced, she began to wander, feeling as if she was moving through a beautiful dream.

The fountain had the elegance of simplicity. There were no ornaments, just a pool with one tall spray rising directly from the water. Donna watched it, revelling in the cool drops that just touched her. At last she turned aside to explore more of the garden.

Here and there were small statues in niches. One in particular caught her attention. It was about three feet high, depicting two boys, one about ten, the other little more than a baby. The older boy was encircling the child with his arm, watching over him with a protective expression. The little one looked out at the world, his arms thrown wide, the hands stretching eagerly to grasp life. Only the older child knew that life could be dangerous as well as beautiful, and his arm stayed firmly in place, warding off evil.

Donna found a shaded stone bench and sat down, glorying in the peace and beauty of her surroundings.

'Yes,' she murmured happily to herself. 'Oh, yes. This is so right, so perfect.'

She closed her eyes and sat a while, listening to the water and the sound of birds. When she opened them again she became aware that she was no longer alone. A man was watching her from the other side of the fountain. At first she had only a hazy impression of a shadow standing behind the huge spray, the details obscured by the cascading water, and the fact that the sun was behind him. He seemed to loom up, a menacing silhouette, perceived like a dream through the glittering droplets. She rubbed her eyes, but he was still there.

He came round the fountain and stood regarding her. There was a puzzled look in his eyes. At last he spoke in a cynical, drawling voice.

'Well?' he said in English. 'Is it as splendid as you'd hoped?'

Now she could see him properly. He was very tall and broad-shouldered. His face was an older version of Toni's, and she knew that this must be his brother, Rinaldo. The dark eyes were the same, so was the high forehead—indeed all the features looked as if they'd come from the same mould, but then something had changed and hardened them. Toni laughed a lot. This man looked as if he never laughed. Toni's wide mouth was made for kissing. The same shape on his brother hinted at a sensuality that was almost cruel.

But one thing was clear to her with almost shocking clarity. Toni was a boy. This was a man.

His expression went with his voice—cool, appraising. 'I'm Rinaldo Mantini,' he said in the same tone. 'Toni's brother.'

'Yes—I guessed,' she said shyly. 'You're so like him.'

A wry grin twisted his mouth. 'Only in appearance, *signorina*. In nature we're not at all alike. Toni is an enthusiast who jumps into life without considering the consequences. As a result he often finds he's been taken in. I'm the opposite. Nobody and nothing fools me.'

She wasn't sure what answer he expected her to make to that. The only thing that was certain was that he wasn't in a welcoming mood. Donna held out her hand.

'I'm Donna Easton,' she said. 'I expect Toni has told you about me—'

He touched her hand for the briefest possible moment, and his features didn't soften. 'Toni has told me all about you,' he confirmed. 'In fact, he's told me far more than he realises.'

She frowned. 'I don't know what you mean by that.'

'Don't you? Well, never mind for the moment. You're here as my brother's bride, and naturally I extend you the welcome of our house.'

But although he spoke of welcome there was no warmth in his tone. Only cold irony.

Donna summoned up her courage and found an irony to match his own. 'Your hospitality overwhelms me,' she said. 'I'd heard that Italians were famous for their kindness to guests, and now I see that it's true.'

For a moment she saw astonishment in his eyes, followed by something that might have been appreciation. Then it was gone. 'Not entirely true,' he said, 'since my brother seems to have left you alone.'

'I have no complaints about your brother's behaviour towards me,' she said firmly, emphasising the word 'brother' very slightly. 'He always treats me well.'

'I'm sure he does. Toni likes to give. He doesn't always give wisely, or to the right person. But his heart is good.' Rinaldo delivered the words with a wry twist of the mouth and a wealth of meaning that left Donna feeling uncomfortable. Her temper began to simmer.

'Toni's told me a great deal about you, as well,' she said. 'He said you were longing for him to marry, and he seemed to think you'd be delighted about us.'

'Toni has always believed what he wants to believe. Whenever he brings his fiancées here, he's always convinced that I'll be pleased.'

Donna stared. 'Fiancées? Plural?'

'You're the fourth—or is it the fifth? I've lost count. The procedure is always the same. He turns up out of the blue with some totally unsuitable female in tow and announces that she's the one. The lady and I have a short conversation, after which she departs a good deal richer than she arrived. My dear girl, you're one of a crowd.'

Donna's temper nearly boiled over at the blatant way he announced his manipulations. 'If you keep blighting his engagements it's no wonder he has so many,' she snapped. 'And if you're suggesting that I'm here to be bought off you can forget it. I love Toni, and he loves me. And we're getting married.'

'Good, good. Don't concede too easily. Put the price up. But there's a limit beyond which I won't go, so don't waste your time trying to push me beyond it.'

'You're mad,' she cried. 'You've got this obsessed way of looking at things, and you can't see the truth.'

'But I have seen the truth,' he replied coolly. 'I saw it on your face a few minutes ago. You surveyed your surroundings like a dealer checking a good investment, and you were delighted with what you discovered.'

'I was delighted with its beauty,' she said, outraged. 'That was all. This garden is one of the loveliest places I've seen. Or it was. Not now. Not with you in it. Now it's like Eden after the serpent invaded.'

He flinched, and she knew she'd said something that had hit home. 'I have to admit that your approach is original,' he said. 'In fact you're not at all like Toni's usual choice in women. The others have all been brazen young pieces, with their charms set out on the stall, ready to bargain. You're more subtle.'

His eyes raked her up and down in a way that made her conscious of her own deficiencies again. 'There's less to please the eye.' His voice was smooth as he uttered this casual cruelty, then added another to it. 'You're also a lot older than his usual girls. Much too old for Toni.'

'I'm three years older than he is, and I've never pretended otherwise,' she said deliberately. 'Maybe he's not the child you seem to think.'

He gave a harsh laugh. 'You mean he's matured? I doubt that.'

'What you think doesn't matter. If you imagine you can talk Toni out of marrying me, you're welcome to try.'

'Look, I've played this scene too often to be interested in the details. Just tell me how much it will take this time. I'll go as high as ten thousand English pounds. I may even go up to twelve thousand if you're reasonable, but the longer you try my patience, the less you'll get.'

His arrogance almost took her breath away. She recovered enough to say, 'You're wasting your time. I don't touch tainted money.'

'Fine talk, but my money is made honestly.'

'But you use it for a tainted purpose,' she flashed. 'You try to buy and sell love—'

'On the contrary. Love has nothing to do with this.'

'How would you know? You couldn't recognise love unless it came with an itemised invoice. I'm marrying Toni because I love him, and also because—' She stopped. This wasn't the moment to speak of the baby. She and Toni must do that together.

'Yes?' he enquired, his eyebrows raised sarcastically.

'I'm marrying him for love,' she repeated. 'His love and mine. And nothing you can do can touch that. You can threaten all you like. The bottom line is that you're helpless.'

In the silence a very ugly look crossed his face. 'You are very brave, *signorina*,' he said at last. 'And also very stupid. I don't allow people to cross me and escape the consequences. It's—bad for business.'

'This isn't business.'

'It's business all right. But I'm better at it than you. A moment ago you'd won a substantial sum. Now you've lost everything, as you'll soon discover.'

'No, *you* will discover that people's feelings can't be bought off so easily.'

'Don't be a little fool,' he said roughly. 'I could turn my brother against you in a moment.'

'If you really thought that you wouldn't have offered me ten thousand pounds.'

His mouth tightened. 'I was trying to conduct our negotiations reasonably—'

'Oh, no, you were trying to bully me. But I can't be bullied, so don't waste your time. Try turning Toni against me. See how far you get.'

'You're very confident,' he said grimly. 'Arrogant even. You'll discover that in this house only one person is allowed to be arrogant.'

But the knowledge of the child she carried gave Donna courage. Toni wanted their baby. He would never turn against his child's mother. So she didn't answer Rinaldo in words. She let her smile say it for her, and she had the satisfaction of seeing the certainty drain away from his face. Their glances met—on one side the timeless certainty of motherhood, linked to the earth and all things eternal, on the other side a dawning unease, mixed with anger and tinged with reluctant respect.

'You have made a very dangerous mistake, *signorina*,' he said softly.

'And you have made a very foolish one,' she replied.

He drew in his breath sharply. But before he could speak they heard a cry from the shadows of the cloisters. The next moment, a very tall, elderly man appeared. He too had the Mantini face, but in him it was thinner, and topped off by a thatch of snow-white hair. Delight radiated from him as he hobbled towards them with the aid of a stick.

'So this is my new granddaughter,' he said. 'Welcome, my dear. Welcome, welcome to our home!'

CHAPTER TWO

A MULTITUDE of emotions warred on Rinaldo's face at this sudden interruption: annoyance at having his rejection of Donna undercut by his grandfather's welcome, the need to disguise his anger in front of the old man, confusion at not receiving support from one he respected. Donna read all these in his expression. In the end propriety won, but it took a huge effort.

'Nonno,' he said courteously, 'this is Signorina Donna Easton, from England. Signorina Easton, this is my grandfather, Piero Mantini.'

'Welcome to the Villa Mantini, my dear child.' The old man bubbled over. Instead of taking Donna's outstretched hand he put his arms about her in an exuberant hug. She hugged him back, overjoyed to receive a welcome at last.

'*Grazie, signore,*' she murmured.

'Why, she speaks our language already,' he beamed.

'Two words,' Rinaldo observed wryly.

'Oh, don't be so grumpy,' his grandfather reproved him. '*Signorina, e felice di essere finalmente qui con noi?*'

Donna just glimpsed the curl of Rinaldo's lip, as though he were saying that now her pretensions would be exposed. But she'd understood Piero's words, asking if she was happy to be there with them at last, and it gave her the greatest satisfaction to reply, '*Molto felice, signore. Desideravo tanto conoscere la familia di Toni.*'

Rinaldo's mouth tightened at her assertion that she'd looked forward to meeting Toni's family. She met his eyes in silent defiance.

It was Toni, standing just behind his grandfather, who broke the tension. 'Donna isn't used to this heat. I'd like to get her inside.'

'Of course, of course,' Piero agreed. 'Maria will show you to your room.' An elderly woman, dressed entirely in black, appeared from the shadows. 'Maria,' Piero said, 'this is Donna who is going to be one of the family soon. Take her upstairs and make her comfortable.'

'I will have your bags sent up,' Rinaldo said formally. 'I hope you will find everything to your liking.'

The room Maria showed her to was enormous, with two tall windows overlooking the front of the house. At this time of day the shutters were drawn, making everything dark. Maria threw them open, giving Donna a view of the large bed, with the headboard made of beautiful polished walnut.

While Maria was displaying the cupboards and the bathroom, there was a knock at the door and a young man entered carrying Donna's bags. He was followed by a maid with a tray.

'Some food and wine for you,' Maria said. 'Rinaldo thought you would wish to have a good, long siesta after your tiring journey.'

She spoke with an air of finality that left no doubt that this was a royal command. Obviously Rinaldo wanted her out of the way while he talked to Toni. But Donna wasn't disposed to argue. She felt weary and hot, and slightly queasy. Also, her mind was disturbed by the discovery of how much Toni had concealed from her. She needed time and peace to think.

She showered and consumed the refreshments, then lay down on the bed for a nap. She woke to the feel of Toni's lips on hers, and put her arms round him, holding onto him as the one point of safety in an alien world.

'My room is right up the other end of the house,' he said with a grin. 'Fancy that, when we're already proud parents-to-be!'

'Have you told anyone?'

'Not yet. I'm waiting for the right moment.'

'Toni, why didn't you tell me about all your other fiancées?'

'*All* my other fiancées?' he teased. 'You make me sound like Bluebeard.'

'Four or five, according to your brother.'

'Oh, they didn't count. Only you count.' His tone showed that he was bored with the subject.

'But you left me without any idea what I was walking into,' Donna protested.

He shrugged. 'Don't make so much of it. We're going to be married, and that's all that matters.'

'I wish you'd be serious for a moment.'

Toni pulled a sulky face. 'If you're going to be serious I shall think you're as bad as Rinaldo.'

'And that's another thing. You said he'd welcome the prospect of your getting married, but he just thinks I'm after your money, like the others. He won't believe that I didn't even know your family was rich. You should have warned me about that too.'

'Why, would it have made you love me better?' he teased.

'Of course not. On the contrary, it would have put me off.'

'Perhaps in my heart I knew that. Besides, I've never felt rich. Rinaldo makes me a beggarly allowance because he wants to force me to come home. I'm always in debt, you know that.'

'I almost can't blame Rinaldo for what he's thinking about me.'

'I can. We've just had a big row. When he saw he couldn't change my mind he got very angry. Nonno came to my rescue. He says there's to be no more arguing over supper tonight.'

'I'm not looking forward to that. Will there be an atmosphere?'

'Don't worry. Selina will be there. She's an old girl-friend of Rinaldo's. Thirteen years ago he was really crazy about her, and they got engaged. Everyone was against it. He was only twenty and she was eighteen, but Rinaldo was determined to have his own way—as he always is—just as soon as he was of age.'

'So what happened?'

'Selina was film mad. She was always hanging around Cinecitta, the film studio in Rome. Somehow she actually managed to meet a film star and get into his bed. The next thing we knew, she'd vanished. It was a month before Rinaldo's twenty-first birthday, and he was planning the wedding, but Selina went off to New York for a fling with this film star. Their pictures were in all the papers, along with the man's wife sobbing and pleading for him to return. Not that Selina would care about that. She thought he could get her into films.'

'And did he?'

'In a way. She thought she'd be a big international star, but she ended up with small parts in minor Italian films. She can't act, but she just had to look gorgeous and say a few words. Now her career's drying up. Her last part was over a year ago.'

'How did Rinaldo take it?' Donna asked. 'He seems like the kind of man who would smash things.'

'Oh, yes. Nonno said he'd never seen a man so much in love, or so angry. I was only eleven at the time, but I knew quite a lot because Rinaldo's rage hung over the house like a black cloud. For a while he went a little crazy. He had a fast car, which he drove at top speed. I'll never know how he didn't have an accident. Then suddenly he stopped. He's like that. Never quite out of control. He sees the danger and says to himself, I won't do this. And he stops.'

Donna gave a little shiver. 'I don't think I like the sound of him. He sounds superhuman—inhuman—*not* human, anyway.'

'His control is superhuman,' Toni agreed. 'When he sets his mind to something it's like watching a laser beam. He went back to work and got on with his life, but no one dared mention Selina's name to him. On the day we heard she'd married a producer everyone crept around, even Nonno, and Rinaldo's face was as black as thunder. Two years later she got divorced and it was in all the papers, but no one said a word to him.'

'But she's here tonight, as a friend?' Donna said.

'Somehow she managed to reappear in Rinaldo's life and they started seeing each other again. She has an apartment on the Via Veneto where the glitzy people live. In all your reading about Italy, have you come across the Via Veneto?'

'Of course I have. *La dolce vita!*' Donna said dramatically.

'That's right. I used to think it was the most thrilling place on earth: the sweet life, delicious wickedness and glamorous sin. All with plenty of money. It's exactly the right place for Selina. Rinaldo visits her, and I suspect he's paying her rent. The producer went bankrupt and her alimony dried up. So Rinaldo helps her financially and she probably repays him in her own way. She's persuaded herself that he's stayed single all these years for love of her.'

'Do you think that's true?'

Toni gave a hoot of laughter. 'What, Rinaldo? Never. The only influence she had was to teach him that no woman can be trusted and most of them are for sale. He's had plenty of women. They throw themselves at his head, and he takes what he wants. But none of them have touched his heart. Rinaldo never makes the same mistake twice, and he doesn't forgive.'

'But he seems to have forgiven her.'

'Don't believe it. He's conducting this affair on his own terms.'

'You mean he sleeps with her and enjoys watching her angling to catch him?'

'It wouldn't surprise me. Maybe he'll marry her in the end, but you can't blame him for enjoying his revenge first.'

Donna shivered again.

When she dressed for the evening she worked hard on her appearance. She would never be glamorous, but she could be elegant. She smiled wryly as she recalled her worries over the cream silk cocktail dress she'd brought. It had once been a designer model, and she'd spent the last of her savings to buy it second-hand, worrying in case it would be too dressy. But in company with a film actress, even a minor one, she would be hard-pressed to hold her own.

Still, she was pleased with the result. The dress was cut away at the throat, without being immodestly low. Around her long neck she wore a single strand of pearls which had been Toni's gift. She tried piling her hair onto her head, but although she liked the more sophisticated air it gave her she decided it would be unwise to underline the fact that she was older than Toni.

He collected her and tucked her arm into his as they went along the corridor. 'You're beautiful,' he said. 'But tomorrow I'm going to buy you an olive-green dress.'

'Why olive-green?' she laughed.

'Because the colour will suit you. Don't argue. I'm never wrong about colours. And I'll give you rubies to go with it.'

'Dreamer!' she chided.

'No, truly. A ruby necklace and ruby earrings. You'll look wonderful.'

Before she could answer Rinaldo appeared round the corner. He nodded politely to them both and went on his way without a word, but Donna realised with dismay that he'd heard Toni's words, and that they would confirm his impression of her. Then her head went up. What did she care what Rinaldo thought?

Downstairs Toni said, 'Let's wait outside, in my mother's garden.'

'Was Loretta your mother?'

'That's right. The courtyard was bare before she started work on it. It was her life's work. She was a sculptress, but she gave it up when she married my *papà*. He didn't want her doing things outside the home.'

'That's outrageous,' Donna said indignantly. 'He sounds like a real tyrant.'

'*Sì*, just like Rinaldo,' Toni said with a laugh. 'So Mamma made this garden, and all the statues in it.'

'I love this one,' Donna said, stopping in front of the bronze of the two boys.

'I wonder if you can guess who they are?' he asked significantly.

'You and your brother?'

'That's right. Rinaldo was ten and I was one when she made this.'

'It's beautiful,' Donna breathed. 'There's real love here. I think your mother must have been a wonderful woman.'

'She was,' Toni said instantly. 'I was only five when she died, but I remember her so well. She was very pretty, and she loved me. I always knew I was her favourite. Papà was an angry man, always losing his temper, but Mamma wouldn't let him be angry with me. Once I stole some *panettone* from the kitchen, and she told him that she'd eaten it so he wouldn't beat me.' Toni laughed at the memory, but immediately his face became shadowed. 'Then she died, and the world was cold.' Then his beaming smile broke out. 'But now I have you, *carissima*, and the world will never be cold again.'

Donna regarded him tenderly. Was this the secret of her attraction for him—the fact that she was a little older, that they'd met when he was her patient, and she was caring for him? She remembered how often he'd said she was like a Madonna, and his words when she'd told him about the child. 'You're going to be a mother...' spoken in a tone of reverence and delight.

And if this was the answer, did it really matter? They were fulfilling each other's needs, and that could be the basis of a very happy marriage. Silently she vowed to love and protect him all her life.

She jumped as a small furry body leapt between them and onto the ledge.

'Hello, Sasha,' Toni cried, stroking the cat. 'She belongs to Nonno Piero. See, she likes you.' Sasha was

making her approval clear, rubbing herself against
Donna and purring like an engine.

'But of course,' came Piero's voice. 'Everybody must
like Donna.'

They waited as he descended the courtyard stairs
towards them, and kissed Donna. 'You will let me take
you in to dinner?' he said. 'Toni won't mind. It's one
of the privileges of age, to be able to steal a pretty girl
from the young men.'

Donna laughed and slipped her arm through his,
grateful to have him on her side.

Rinaldo was in the salon that looked out onto the
patio. He was dressed in a dinner jacket, with a snow-
white shirt and a black bow tie. His handsome, imperious head towered above everyone else's, and drew
Donna's reluctant admiration. Even Toni's good looks
were thrown into the shade next to his brother's arrogant grandeur. But this was a man on his home ground,
a panther defending his cave, and woe betide intruders!

Beside Rinaldo was a tall woman with long blonde
hair and a skin-tight black dress. The neck was daringly
low, the waist tight and the hem short, revealing long,
lovely legs sheathed in black silk. About her neck hung
a diamond necklace, diamond pendants swung from her
ears, and more diamonds flashed on her wrists. She
swayed towards them, wafting a very expensive perfume
as she went.

'Toni, darling,' she cried, enveloping him in her embrace, 'it's so good to have you back here. We mustn't
let you run away again, must we, Rinaldo?'

She appealed theatrically to the older brother, but he
shrugged prosaically and said, 'Toni never takes any
notice of anything I say.'

Toni disengaged himself. 'You must meet Donna, my fiancée,' he said. 'Donna, this is Selina, an old family friend.'

Only by the swiftest flash of her eyes did Selina betray that she disliked the description. The next moment she embraced Donna effusively.

'Why, Toni, darling, she's charming,' she cried, speaking over Donna's head, as if she weren't really there. 'I just adore that quiet, demure look.' She beamed a diamond smile at Donna. 'How clever of you not to attempt anything showy. One should know one's own style, don't you think?'

'Know my place, you mean?' Donna murmured.

Rinaldo was just close enough to hear. A tremor passed over his face, but he controlled it instantly. Their eyes met. Despite his antagonism Donna felt he'd been briefly on her side.

Toni gave a shout of laughter. 'Do you know, Donna calls herself a little brown mouse?' he said. 'But don't you believe it.' He tapped Donna's forehead lightly. 'She's got brains in there. More than me.'

'Anyone has more brains than you,' Rinaldo observed drily.

Donna smiled. 'At this moment I'd sacrifice brains if I could look like you,' she told Selina pleasantly. 'No one could mistake you for a little brown mouse.'

Selina made a self-deprecating gesture, honed and polished to perfection. 'Looks are nothing,' she declared gaily. 'It's all the effect of the diamonds. I tell Rinaldo he gives me too many, but he just won't stop.'

Selina turned her attentions onto Piero. Rinaldo regarded Donna with narrowed eyes, behind which interest gleamed. 'I'm not just empty words, you see,' he murmured. 'I know how to be generous.'

'Well, some men prefer to express themselves with money,' Donna said pointedly. She met his eyes. 'And some know no other way.'

'I dare say you could tell me about that.'

'Your brother is different, *signore*. He gives his heart.'

'*Signore?*' he asked ironically. 'If you're planning to become part of this family, shouldn't you be calling me by my name?'

'I doubt whether you and I could ever be part of the same family—not in any way that means anything. Toni, yes. Your grandfather, yes. But not us.'

'Showing your claws, eh?'

'You declared your enmity for me in the first moments,' she told him in a soft, angry voice. 'At least that's honest. Remain my enemy, *signore*. Then I know where I stand.'

'So you carry the fight into the heart of the enemy's camp,' he said. 'Courageous, but futile. I sympathise with a forlorn hope.'

'Perhaps not as forlorn as you think,' she riposted, smiling. 'How do you know I don't have a secret weapon?'

'I shall wait with trepidation.'

'Now are we all ready to go in to dinner?' Piero asked, shepherding everyone. With Donna on his arm he led the way into the dining room. It was a long room, one of whose walls was almost entirely given up to floor-length windows that opened onto the cloister. Light poured in from this side, throwing the rest of the room into shade.

After a while Donna's eyes grew accustomed to it, and she saw that the dining room was traditional, but quietly luxurious. The table and chairs were made of dark wood.

The chairs had very tall backs, covered with tapestry, as were the seats.

The table was laid with silver and gleaming crystal. Three glasses of different sizes and shapes stood like soldiers beside each place. They looked so fragile—as if a breath might cause them to shatter.

Piero indicated her place and pulled out a chair for her. She found herself seated in the middle of one of the long sides of the table, with Rinaldo directly opposite her. To her relief Toni was beside her. Under the table he gave her hand a gentle squeeze, and she squeezed back, trying to convey how nervous she was.

Donna noticed that the chair on Piero's far side was unoccupied, and wondered who was to join them. Then Piero gave a little whistle, and his cat scuttled across the floor and leapt onto the chair.

'Sasha likes to eat with me,' Piero declared.

Selina tittered. 'What a sweet idea! But then, you're a very sweet pussy, aren't you, *carissima*?'

Sasha hissed at her. Selina quickly drew back the hand she'd held out to stroke the furry head.

Rinaldo eyed his grandfather with fond exasperation. 'Since everybody is now present, perhaps we can begin,' he said.

Maria appeared. She was still wearing black, but now her dress was of silk, indicating that she was going to supervise the serving of the meal.

'Maria has prepared a very special meal in your honour,' Rinaldo told Donna with a little inclination of his head.

'That—that was very kind of her,' Donna said awkwardly. The luxury was beginning to oppress her, and her poise seemed to have drained away through the soles of her feet.

Under Maria's direction two maids appeared, bearing bottles. They went down the table filling the largest glasses with sparkling mineral water and the next size with dry white wine. When Maria was satisfied that this had been done properly she gave them a brief nod and they scurried away, returning a moment later with trolleys bearing the first course, which she served herself.

Donna had often eaten in Italian restaurants, but this was her first experience of Italian food cooked on its home ground, and it was overwhelming. To start with there was aubergine salad—a mixture of diced aubergine, celery, olives and endives, served with slices of hard-boiled egg and flavoured with onion, garlic and something that tasted incredibly like bitter chocolate.

Toni laughed when he saw her face. 'Yes, it's chocolate,' he said. 'It's a special trick of Maria's to put a little in with the vinegar.'

'It's the most unbelievable taste,' Donna said. 'Maria must be a genius.'

When Maria appeared, to supervise the clearing of the plates, Piero repeated this, to her obvious pleasure.

'*Grazie, signorina,*' she said, smiling at Donna.

There followed a dish of tagliatelle with pumpkin, which was even more delicious. Donna began to wonder how she could eat any more, yet such was Maria's skill that the two previous dishes balanced each other, leaving her satisfied but not satiated.

'For the main course Maria has prepared roast leg of lamb, especially for you,' Rinaldo informed her. 'She believes the English cannot be happy without roast lamb.'

But this was like no roast lamb Donna had ever encountered on an English table. It appeared on a bed of garlic, celery, onions and carrots, and was lavishly spiced with rosemary and oregano. Somewhere, too, Donna detected the taste of wine. It was more than a meal. It was a work of art.

Red wine was poured to go with the lamb. Maria frowned at the sight of Donna's white wine, which she had barely touched.

'You do not like wine, *signorina*?' Rinaldo asked.

'I prefer mineral water,' Donna said. In fact she normally enjoyed wine, but she avoided alcohol now she knew that she was pregnant.

'Signorina Easton wants to keep her wits about her,' Selina said with a touch of mischief. 'She probably feels that she's in the lion's den.'

'But how can that be, when she is the guest of honour?' Rinaldo enquired silkily.

'Perhaps, *signore*, because you remind me of a Roman emperor,' Donna replied. 'Didn't some of them used to invite their enemies to dine, treat them with honour, and then—' she made an expressive gesture with her hands '—the enemies were never seen again? Who knows what became of them?'

Toni grinned, and Piero shouted with laughter. 'What do you say to that?' he demanded of his grandson. 'A Roman emperor.' He turned to Donna. 'Now you must say which one. Nero? Caligula?'

'Neither of them,' Donna said. 'They were mad and stupid, and I'm sure that whatever Signor Rinaldo does is done with intention, and worked out beforehand to the last detail, with no concession to emotion.'

'Then who?' Piero begged eagerly. He was enjoying himself.

'Augustus, perhaps?' Donna suggested.

Piero nodded. 'A chilly, unfeeling devil. There, Rinaldo. She has you to perfection. But how do you come to know so much about our history?'

Rinaldo's smile was deadly. 'I think you'll find, Nonno, that Signorina Easton has also worked out everything to the last detail—with no concession to emotion.'

'You speak as if you know her well,' Selina said, her glance flashing, cat-like, between them.

'I think perhaps I do,' Rinaldo agreed.

The look in his eyes seemed to reach across the table and scorch Donna. But she wasn't afraid. The knowledge that she could take this man by surprise was like heady wine.

'But she's a stranger to all of us,' Selina complained. 'Tell us about yourself, *Signorina.*'

'There's very little to tell. I'm a nurse. I met Toni when he crashed his car and was brought to the hospital where I work.'

'But how romantic!' Selina exclaimed. 'And did you fall in love instantly?'

'Yes,' Toni said. 'Donna is my own private angel of mercy.'

'And your family?' Rinaldo asked. 'How do they feel about your marriage?'

'I have no family to speak of,' Donna said abruptly. 'My mother is dead. My father left home years ago. These days I hardly know him.'

'She wouldn't even take me to meet him,' Toni said with a laugh. 'I think he must be some kind of ogre.'

Selina's eyes glinted. 'Well, we all have relations that we don't want people to meet.'

Donna's mouth tightened. It was true that she'd refused to take Toni to visit her father. She couldn't face him seeing how uninterested her own father was in her. But Selina's words had implied something else, something shabby.

'That's perfectly true,' Piero announced. 'None of my relations ever want people to meet me. I'm the family skeleton. Have been for years.'

In the general laugh that this evoked the moment passed. Piero fed Sasha another titbit, apparently oblivious to having defused the tension. Donna saw Rinaldo frowning, and realised that another black mark had been notched against her. A woman without family, who would gain honour from her marriage but bring none to her husband.

The maids appeared and cleared the plates. Maria served chilled zabaglione, made of egg yolks whisked with Marsala wine, and decorated with amaretti biscuits. Like everything else in the meal it was perfectly prepared, and precisely calculated to set off what had gone before.

Then there was coffee in tiny porcelain cups, and brandy for those who wanted it. Piero stood up. 'And now I want to propose a toast,' he said.

Rinaldo looked puzzled. Selina fixed a smile on her face, but Piero gave no sign of noticing them. He beamed at Toni, then at Donna.

'This is a happy day,' he said. 'Our Toni has brought home a bride who will truly be worthy of this house. It will be our pleasure to make her a part of the family.' He raised his glass. 'I drink to my new granddaughter.'

The others all drank. Toni smiled at Donna.

'And there is one more thing,' Piero added to Donna. 'I have a special gift for you.' He reached into his pocket and brought out a tiny object, which he held up.

'This ring has been in the Mantini family for generations. I gave it to my wife, and it stayed on her finger until the day she died. Traditionally the eldest son has given it to his bride, but since Rinaldo refuses to marry

I give it to you, dear child, to show that you will be a true Mantini.'

He took her right hand and slipped the ring onto the third finger. It was a beautiful thing, made of emeralds and rubies, with an exotic design. Donna gasped with delight, less at its obvious value than at its symbol of welcome. For a moment tears blurred her eyes. When they cleared she saw Rinaldo's face, a mask of fury. She understood. She'd not only stolen his brother, but also part of his inheritance.

But after the first moment of anger he concealed his feelings, smiling and congratulating her. Selina did less well. Her mouth made the right movements but her eyes were cold, and Donna guessed she'd seen the ring as one day belonging to herself.

The rest of the evening passed uneventfully. Selina departed in a cloud of perfume and blown kisses. Rinaldo escorted her to her car. Toni poured his grandfather another drink, and Donna slipped out into the courtyard.

It was blessedly cool outside, besides being a relief to escape from the house. High up, trapped in the oblong of the buildings, the moon gleamed, illuminating everything below in silver. By its light Donna wandered over to the fountain and sat on the side, listening to the falling of the water and looking into the depths. Now and then a curious goldfish broke the surface, gazed at her and disappeared. She waggled a finger in the water, laughing softly as the goldfish darted in all directions.

Some changed quality in the air made her look up suddenly. Rinaldo was watching her, his face hidden in shadow. She wondered how long he'd been there.

He came towards her. He had a brandy glass in each hand, and he offered one to her.

'No, thank you,' she said instantly.

'It's good brandy,' he said, seating himself by the side of the pool, so that he could see her. 'The best. I don't offer it to everyone.'

'I'm honoured, but I never drink spirits,' she said firmly.

'You're a most unexpected woman. I'll admit that you've totally taken me by surprise.'

'But not enough to make you trust my motives?'

'On the contrary, I distrust you more than ever now I know how well you've prepared yourself to become part of this household.'

'But I didn't— Oh, why bother, when you don't believe me?'

'True, why bother? If it comes to that, why does a woman like you bother with a boy like Toni?'

'Because he's kind and sweet-natured,' she said, looking him in the eye. 'And because he wants me.'

'And you? What do you want?'

'I want—' her voice wavered suddenly '—I want to belong.'

Why had she said that? she wondered. She didn't know, except that there was something in this man's force of personality that compelled the truth.

He was looking at her curiously. 'And you think you will belong here?'

'If you will let me.'

'But I will not let you. You don't belong here as Toni's wife, and I won't allow you to fool yourself, or him.' He seized her hand suddenly. 'Listen to me,' he said in a low, urgent voice. 'If it's security you want, I'll give it to you. You can have an apartment in the most luxurious part of Rome, jewellery, clothes, anything you want—at my expense. I have friends who will give you a job to pass the time. All I ask is that you always be ready for me when I want you.'

She stared at him in horror. 'I don't believe what I'm hearing.'

'I only half believe it myself,' he said grimly. 'But I'll do anything to prevent the tragedy you're planning.'

She pulled her hand free. The physical contact with him unnerved her. 'And what about Toni's feelings? Don't you care about them?'

'It's because I care about him that I'm going to stop this marriage.'

'I belong to Toni.'

'You'll never belong to him in a million years,' Rinaldo said fiercely. 'And you know it. You've known it from the moment we met.'

'You arrogant—'

'Don't waste time calling me names because of what neither of us can help.'

'It's not true,' she said fiercely.

'Isn't it?' he asked, looking deep into her eyes. The next moment he lifted his hand and trailed his fingertips gently down the side of her face.

The sensation shattered her. His touch was feather-light, but it sent tremors through her in a way Toni's touch had never done. The whole world seemed to spin.

'Toni is a boy,' Rinaldo said softly. 'And you're not a girl but a woman. You need a man.'

'But not you,' she said, speaking with difficulty. 'Never you.'

'Why not me? Why not a man who can appreciate you, instead of that sulky child who wants you to mother him? Toni will forget. But we—we won't forget.'

Through the roaring in her ears she clung to one thought—that this was an unscrupulous man who'd stop at nothing to separate her from his brother. Even if it meant seducing her himself. But when the break was final he would toss her aside.

She fought to remind herself of this while his touch delighted and tormented her. She tried to pull away but his eyes held her in a hypnotic trance. His fingertips moved to her mouth, and slowly he began to trace the outline of her lips. The sensation was overwhelming. She hadn't known her flesh could experience such feelings. He was making her discover desires that she knew she should shun, forcing her to acknowledge that behind their mutual antagonism lay another feeling, far more dangerous than hostility.

Her mouth burned with the longing to feel his mouth against it. She couldn't breathe. She wanted this to stop. She wanted it to go on for ever.

'Only say yes,' he whispered, 'and I will do whatever is necessary. I'll take you away from here tonight and you need never see Toni again.'

She drew a long, shuddering breath, trying to still the mad pounding of her heart. The mention of Toni's name had the effect of reviving her courage. Toni loved her. He would be broken-hearted at what his brother was trying to do to him.

'Take your hands off me,' she said deliberately.

She saw the shock in his face. He'd thought he had her in his trap, and the discovery that she'd escaped brought a flare of anger to his eyes.

'What would Toni say if he knew the truth about you?' she demanded.

'And what, in your opinion, is the truth?'

'That you're the kind of man who tries to seduce his brother's woman.'

He flinched and his face became cruel. 'See if you can make. him believe it.'

'Of course you'd deny it?'

'Of course. There's nothing I won't do to protect my family from danger—*nothing at all*. You've been warned. I would have played fair if you'd been sensible. You'd have had your apartment, and all the rest—as long as it suited me. But you chose to be clever. Well, we'll see who's cleverest.'

He rose abruptly and strode back to the house. Donna remained where she was, shaken. For a moment the look in his eyes, and a certain vibrant note in his voice, had transfixed her. She could almost have forgotten everything else. She shuddered with horror at herself.

Toni came to find her. 'Are you all right?' he asked anxiously. 'Has Rinaldo been making himself unpleasant?'

'No, I'm fine,' she said. 'But I would like to go to bed. I'm very tired.'

Toni took her indoors. Piero kissed her goodnight, and even Sasha came to rub herself against Donna's ankles. There was no sign of Rinaldo.

In her room she closed the door firmly behind her and stood for a moment leaning against it. The shutters were open, and the moonlight revealed something lying on her bed. She put on the light and examined it.

It was a large envelope, stuffed with English money. Appalled, Donna tipped it onto the bed, realising that there was a full ten thousand pounds. There was also a note that said simply, 'For God's sake, take this and go. R!'

CHAPTER THREE

EVEN at night the heat was stifling. Donna tossed and turned before throwing off all the bedclothes, but still there was little relief. She couldn't sleep. A fierce resentment at Rinaldo's behaviour seethed within her, destroying all peace.

Her dreams of being welcomed in Italy, of finally belonging somewhere, were shattered. One cruel, prejudiced man had ruined everything. She hated him.

Then the memory of that moment in the garden came over her again, causing the blood to throb in her veins. The sheer force of Rinaldo's masculinity had made her recognise, for the first time, that she'd tied herself to a young man who hadn't fully grown up, who might never grow up. It made no difference that she hated Rinaldo. Hatred could be as thrilling as love. In fact, more so. Had there ever been one moment when Toni's love had truly thrilled her? She felt gratitude and tenderness towards him, but not the searing awareness that had swept along her nerves in that shattering instant with his brother. She'd told herself that gentle affection would be enough, and she'd believed it, but that was before she had known...

She sat up in bed, shaking her head to clear it of the tormenting vision. She mustn't allow herself to think like that. She loved Toni. No matter that it was the wrong kind of love. It was too late to think of that. He was the father of her child. She forced herself to remember his tender kindness, his pride in her, the way he made her feel cherished. But why hadn't he told the family about the baby?

The thought flickered across her mind that he'd kept silent for fear of Rinaldo. She dismissed the idea, but it left a footprint of unease. Toni feared Rinaldo as a youngster might fear a stern father. It was a troubling thought.

She got up, as oppressed by her own fears as by the heat, flung open the windows and drank in gulps of air. The night was in its last hour of darkness before dawn began to break.

She pulled on her thin cotton dressing gown and slipped out of her room. Somewhere there must be a way out of the house so that she could walk in the garden and grow really cool. She groped around uselessly for a while, before seeing a thin crack of moonlight under a door. Opening it, she found to her relief that she was on the stone staircase that led down into the cloisters. She descended halfway, then sat on the stairs and leaned against the wall, closing her eyes and letting the air waft gently over her. It was blissful.

She almost dozed off in that position. Then she heard the sound of angry Italian voices, deep in the house. In another moment a door was flung open and Toni came storming out into the courtyard.

Rinaldo was close behind him. 'Don't walk away when I'm talking to you,' he snapped.

'I've listened to you for hours,' Toni said.

'I haven't even started yet.'

The brothers had come to a halt near the fountain. Peering through the balustrades, Donna could see them clearly limned by the moonlight. They were still in the clothes they'd worn for dinner, as though they'd fought all night, with neither winning. Rinaldo had taken his jacket off, and torn open the neck of his elegant white shirt. His chest was rising and falling with the force of his anger.

'There are things I'm going to say, and you're going to listen,' he said in a quieter voice.

'I've heard them all before,' Toni said wearily. 'I know I've been a fool in the past, but Donna is different.'

Rinaldo gave a short, scornful laugh. 'You think every girl is different.'

Donna glanced wildly up the stairs whence she'd come. If only she could creep back to her room without being seen. One half of her wanted to stay here and listen while Toni defended her, but the other half shrank from eavesdropping. Besides, suppose she was caught? She shivered at the thought of Rinaldo's contempt if he found her here.

Moving slowly, she began to slide backwards, but her slippers made a faint scratching noise against the stone, and she froze.

'What was that?' Rinaldo demanded, looking round.

'What?' Toni asked impatiently.

'I thought I heard a noise.'

The brothers stood in silence for a moment, while Donna's heart thumped so hard she was sure they must discover her. But at last Toni said, 'The night's full of noises. It was probably Sasha hunting mice. Never mind that.'

'Yes, let's return to this woman who's cast a spell over you,' said Rinaldo in a hard voice. *Dio mio*, I've never seen you so stupid and obstinate before.'

'Because she's different,' Toni said. 'Can't you see that?'

'I can see that she *looks* different,' Rinaldo conceded. 'She's not flashy, but don't be taken in by her demure appearance. She's clever and shrewd. There's an educated brain working behind that pale face.'

'That's it!' Toni rounded on his brother. 'You can't imagine that an educated woman could be interested in me—'

'I find it hard,' Rinaldo admitted grimly. 'In a short life you've made yourself notable for many things—fast cars, expensive tastes, brushes with the law. But brains—never!'

'Think what you like. Donna loves me.'

'She loves your family's money, that's all. You heard her tonight. A woman with no background, three years your senior. You must have seemed like a golden chance, and she seized it. Then you brought her down here and she caught sight of the real goodies. I wish you'd seen her face as she surveyed this garden. She thought she'd found her crock of gold at last.'

'You think the worst of everyone,' Toni said.

'The worst is usually true.'

Toni gave a sudden crack of laughter. 'She stood up to you. That's what you don't like.'

'I've never denied that I think her intelligent, but I tell you this—you two could never be happy together. Now be sensible. You've made a fool of yourself, but it can be made right; I can get rid of her quickly and discreetly.'

'Damn you! Stop trying to pull my strings like a puppet!' Toni said furiously. 'It's always been the same. Toni, do this, do that, until I couldn't breathe.'

'It was as well one of us had a sense of responsibility,' Rinaldo said grimly, 'or your life would have been a disaster by now. I promised our mother that I would take care of you, and that's been a sacred trust to me.'

Toni's voice suddenly went up a pitch, as though Rinaldo had touched a raw nerve. 'Don't speak of our mother,' he shouted. 'Leave her sacred memory out of your dirty scheming.'

'I must speak of her,' Rinaldo snapped. 'It was she who made this family a *family*, who warded off danger and evil from her children. What would she say now if I stood aside while you ruined your life?'

Toni flung his glass away and it shattered against the stone. 'She would know that I'm not ruining my life but saving it,' he shrieked. 'She would be glad for me.' His voice rose again as though he were lashing himself into the courage to speak. 'She would say I was doing the right thing *because a man should marry the mother of his child.*'

In the terrible silence that followed, the words seemed to hang in the air. Donna inched her way along the stair until she could look between the banisters, and saw Rinaldo. Now she understood why Toni was frightened of him. His face was black with anger.

'Did I understand you correctly?' he said at last in a voice of cold menace.

Toni took a step back and his voice shook. But he'd come too far to stop now. 'Donna is pregnant,' he said huskily.

Full of tension, Donna waited for what Rinaldo would say next. But the sound that came from him wasn't made up of words. It was simply a bellow of fury, frustration, and thwarted will. She read all these things in the noise, and in the way he slammed his fist down on the stone.

'You *fool*!' he raged. 'You gullible, credulous fool! She's taken you in with that old trick. I thought even you had more sense. You don't imagine it's yours, do you? How long did it take your angelic Madonna to get pregnant?'

'W-well—almost at once,' Toni stammered, 'but—'

'Of course! She wasted no time once she'd lured you into her bed.'

'She—she didn't lure me—' Toni faltered. 'It took all my pleading before—'

'Oh, maidenly reluctance as well. My God, I underestimated her!'

'You certainly did,' Donna agreed, in English.

Both men swung round to face the stairs, from which Donna rose like an avenging fury. She ran down and faced Rinaldo, too angry to be afraid of him.

'My child is Toni's,' she cried, 'and that's true, no matter how you try to dirty it.'

'I might have known you'd go creeping about my house, eavesdropping,' he sneered.

'I never meant to. I came out here to get cool, and I'm glad now that I did. I think you must be an evil man. You know nothing about me, but you assume the worst, because you prefer to believe the worst of people. Yes, I slept with Toni, because I love him. Now I'm going to have his child. That's something that you can't take away from either of us.'

Emboldened by her defiant spirit, Toni had come to stand beside her, his hand on her shoulder. Rinaldo looked from one to the other, and his face grew ugly. 'Very pretty words,' he snapped. 'But they mean nothing. I don't believe you.'

Donna confronted him head-on. 'To hell with what you believe,' she said simply.

He drew his breath in sharply. His eyes glittered and she could almost feel his fury vibrating in the air about her. Then he muttered an oath and slammed one fist into the other. The next moment he turned on his heel and strode off into the shadows. They heard the crash of a door slamming.

Toni breathed out. 'Oh, Santa Maria!' he muttered. 'I was afraid of how he'd take it, but I didn't think it would be as bad as that!'

'What does it matter?' she pleaded. 'We don't need him. We don't need anyone. The sooner we're away from here the better.'

Without waiting for him to say any more she ran back up the stairs, hurried to her room and began to toss her things into suitcases. She had to get away from this house where she was treated like an enemy.

Toni appeared. '*Cara*, what are you doing?' he asked in dismay when he saw her.

'I'm doing what I said I'd do. Leaving,' she said tersely.

'But you can't leave me!' he cried. 'I need you—'

'Look at this!' She held up the money. 'He tried to pay me off. And look what he dared to write to me!'

Toni stared at the note, then at the money. Dazed, he counted it. 'Do you see how much is here?' he breathed.

'What difference does it make how much it is?' Donna demanded angrily. 'Did you think I'd let him buy me off?'

'Of course not, but—'

Donna didn't wait for him to finish, but began stuffing the notes back into the envelope. She wrote Rinaldo's name on the outside and put it down on her pillow.

'The maid will find that and take it to him in the morning,' she said. 'Now I'm going. I don't want to see him again.'

He seized her hands. 'You're right. We'll both go.'

'I don't want to come between you and your family—'

'But you are my family,' he insisted. 'You and our little *bambino*. We'll go together. Wait while I pack some clothes.'

He vanished, and Donna sat down on the bed, suddenly tired. She'd been in such a temper that she hadn't stopped to think how she would manage if Toni didn't come too.

She felt as if she'd been through a wringer. She had to get away from this cruel place, but most of all she had to get away from Rinaldo Mantini.

Toni was back in a few minutes with a hastily packed bag. 'Ready?' he asked.

'There's one final thing,' she told him. 'Please, darling, try to understand. I can't take your grandfather's ring.'

'But of course you can. He wanted you to have it.'

'It's a family ring—'

'But he gave it to us,' Toni said sulkily.

'I'm sorry, I just can't take it.' Donna slid the beautiful ring off her finger and looked about her. 'Where will it be safe to leave this?' she mused.

'Put it in the envelope with the money,' Toni suggested. 'Here, I'll do it while you check the bathroom.'

'I've checked it.'

'Better do it again. Women always leave something behind, like hairspray or nail polish.'

'All right, all right. But we must be quick.'

In fact Toni's instinct was correct; she'd left her sponge bag by the basin. While she was gathering it up and having a final glance round she heard him say urgently, 'Hurry, I think the house is beginning to stir.'

She emerged from the bathroom. 'Is everything—?'

He grabbed her hand and drew her to the door.
'Listen,' he said softly.

She listened, but could hear nothing.

'Let's go while we can,' he murmured.

Donna followed him out into the corridor. Quietly they
crept to the head of the stairs and began to go slowly
down the broad steps, holding their breath. To her relief
there was no need to go out by the front door. Toni led
her to a side door that opened directly into the garage.
In a few moments they'd loaded up his car and he had
the garage doors open.

Dawn was beginning to break as they drove slowly
down the long path to the front gate. Donna kept looking
behind her, certain that any moment she would find
Rinaldo in pursuit. But nothing happened, and at last
they were on the road. Toni promptly gunned the car
into life, and in a few seconds they were streaking away.
Donna was devoutly thankful to put the Villa Mantini
behind her. She hoped she would never have to see it
again.

They drove for a while in silence, while the land about
them grew lighter by the minute.

Toni gave a sudden shout of laughter. 'Rinaldo's face
when you rose up from the stairs and he realised you'd
heard everything,' he said in a shaking voice. 'I've never
seen him knocked sideways like that.'

'He wasn't too startled to insult me, though, was he?'
Donna asked grimly.

'Oh, he didn't mean anything by it,' he said carelessly.

Donna felt dizzy at Toni's mercurial moods. The relief
of escape seemed to have blown his cares away, and it
was as if the past hour had not existed. 'Toni, he ac-
cused me of trying to pass another man's child off on

you,' she said, with more of an edge to her voice than she'd ever used with him before.

'So what? I didn't believe it.'

'But he had no right to say it. Is he going to throw more mud at me at our wedding?'

'He won't get the chance. We'll marry first and tell him afterwards.'

'We'll do no such thing,' Donna said. 'He'd love that. A hole-and-corner wedding, so that he could tell everyone I'd proved his worst fears. We'll marry in the face of all the world, and send him an invitation. Let him do his worst.'

Instantly Toni's mood changed. The carefree look vanished from his face. '*Cara*, you don't know what Rinaldo's worst is,' he said in a hollow voice. 'He can't bear being defied. He'll do anything to get his own way.'

'What *can* he do?'

'Lots of things. Kidnap me from the church, probably.'

'Be serious.'

'I *am* being serious. Rinaldo has friends who'd do it, for a price.'

Donna stared at him. Toni was watching the road ahead, but she could see by the troubled frown on his face that he wasn't joking. She'd known that Rinaldo was an imperious, arrogant and unscrupulous man. Now she realised that he was also a frightening one. Toni was afraid of him. That much was clear.

'Which way are we going?' she asked.

'I'm heading for the *autostrada*. We're going home.'

'Home? But this is your home.'

'I mean England. We'll vanish where he can't find us.'

'Toni, you don't mean that.'

'Oh, yes, I do! I thought things were going to be so different. I thought Rinaldo would like you, and welcome you into the family. It would have made things so much easier—'

'You mean I could have protected you from him?' Donna asked shrewdly.

Toni just shrugged.

She felt a little stab of dismay. It didn't matter, she told herself. She'd known that Toni was immature. But it *did* matter. That was the truth.

'I'd better fill the tank first,' he muttered, with his eye on the gauge. 'There's a petrol station just up here.'

He swung in and pulled to a halt. While he was filling up Donna got out of the car. Her mind was in turmoil, and she knew she couldn't travel any further with Toni until they'd had a serious talk.

'I need some coffee,' she said. 'There's a little café just opening up over there.'

'All right, but don't let's be too long.'

Like many Italian men Toni liked to carry his immediate possessions in a leather bag worn on a long strap from the shoulder. He pulled this from the car now and followed her into the café.

'Sit there while I get you something,' he said.

Donna sat down and closed her eyes, feeling shaken by everything she'd been through. It didn't seem possible that only yesterday she'd travelled this road full of joy and hope for the future. Now everything was ruined.

No, not everything. She placed a gentle hand over her stomach. She still had her baby, even if she'd become disillusioned with its father. For the sake of her child she would do anything.

Toni returned with coffee and rolls, and gave her his old charming smile. She tried to remind herself that he was still the dear, warm-hearted boy that she loved. When they were away from this place everything would be all right again.

She put a hand out to steady his shoulder bag, which he'd dumped carelessly on a chair. But she was too late and the bag went spilling onto the floor. Toni made a nervous grab at it, but he wasn't fast enough.

'Oh, heavens!' Donna breathed, picking up something that had fallen out. 'How could you do this?'

'Look, *cara*, I was going to explain—'

'This is the money Rinaldo tried to force me to take, isn't it?' she said in disbelieving anger. 'I told you I didn't want it, but you picked it up when my back was turned.'

'Come on, don't make a fuss—'

'A fuss? You knew how I felt about taking his money—'

'Well, we're going to need money.'

'Not *his* money,' she said fiercely. 'Anyone but his.'

'What's wrong with his money? It's as good as anyone else's. He's my brother. Why shouldn't he help us?'

'Because it's deception, can't you understand that?'

But looking into his eyes she saw that he didn't understand at all. It was Toni's nature to take the easiest way. Donna began to feel sick again. She clutched the envelope hard, trying to decide what to do, and felt another pang of dismay as her fingers detected a small, hard bulge.

'What's this?' she asked in dawning horror.

But she knew what it was even before she pulled out Piero's ring. She closed her eyes. 'I explained why I couldn't keep this,' she said desperately.

'Well, I don't see why you shouldn't have it,' he said sulkily. 'Nonno gave it to you.'

'To welcome me into the family, but we're running away. Besides, he should have given it to Rinaldo. He's the eldest son.'

'He could do what he liked with it,' Toni said with an exasperated sigh that showed clearly how all this moralising was getting him down. 'He gave it to us. Can't you see that we're independent now?'

'Independent? With Rinaldo's money and Piero's ring, neither of which we're supposed to have?'

'Well, I think it's rather a good joke to use Rinaldo's money, when he thought he was buying you off. How I wish I could see his face when he finds out!'

'No, you don't,' Donna said with bitter realisation. 'You wouldn't like to be anywhere near when he finds out. Your kind of courage is in secret. You tricked me into checking the bathroom just to get me out of the way while you took all this. Oh, how could you?'

'I was only looking after you,' he said, aggrieved. 'We'll need money to live on until we're married. Then I'm sure Nonno will make me an allowance.'

'An allowance?' she echoed. 'Are you going to go all your life supported by someone else? Toni, I can't live like that.'

'Oh, don't make a fuss,' he said irritably. 'What's wrong with it, anyway? It's family money.'

'It's a family firm, but you're not working in it, are you?'

He shrugged. Donna stared at him in a kind of horror.

They drank their coffee in silence. Her mind was seething with miserable thoughts. 'What did Rinaldo mean about brushes with the law?' she asked after a while.

'Why bring that up now?'

'Because I never heard of it before. What happened?'

'It was nothing. I got followed by a police car when I was speeding and it became a chase. The police car crashed.'

'Good God! Was anyone hurt?'

'No, I promise you. The police got out, swearing at me, but their car was a write-off.'

'How long ago was this?'

'About six months, just before I went to England.'

'You mean you escaped to England before you were charged?' Donna asked. The pieces were falling into place quickly now.

'Rinaldo said I should lie low while he made it all right. He called about a month later and said it was safe to go home, but by that time I'd met you, *cara*.' He gave her his old winning smile, but she'd seen the weakness behind it and it didn't touch her heart as it once had done.

'No wonder Rinaldo was against me from the start,' she murmured.

With sudden resolution she drained her coffee, stuffed the envelope into her bag, and got up. 'Come along,' she told him, and began to walk towards the car, Toni trotting obediently after her.

'Hey, I'll drive,' he protested as she got into the driver's seat.

'I'll drive,' she said. She didn't want an argument about what she was going to do. She started the engine and swung the car round.

'Where are you going?' Toni yelped. 'This is the wrong way.'

'It's the right way. We're going back.'

'*What*? Are you crazy? Do you know how mad he'll be?'

'Toni, can't you see that we have to go back and return the money and the ring? They're not ours. I won't keep them under false pretences.'

'OK, OK, we'll send them back through the post the next time we stop. Now turn the car round.'

'We can't send such valuable things through the post. Besides, I want to see Rinaldo's face when I hand them over and tell him what he can do with his money.'

'His face is just what I don't want to see,' Toni groaned.

Donna spoke instinctively. 'Don't worry, I'll look after you.'

Instead of being indignant at the suggestion that he needed her protection Toni groaned again. 'You think you will, but you haven't seen Rinaldo when he's in a really nasty temper. For God's sake, turn round!'

'No!'

'Look, we'll get married, then we can go back and see him.'

'No,' she repeated stubbornly. And even as she spoke she knew that there would be no wedding. Even for her child's sake she couldn't marry Toni. There would be no peace, always wondering what this overgrown infant was lying about or evading. She would let him see his child as often as he wanted, but it would be madness to chain her life to his. She should have seen it long ago.

She focused on the road ahead, longing for the moment when she would return to the Villa Mantini, hurl Rinaldo's money at him and depart, a free woman.

'Donna, you've *got* to turn back.'

'I'm going to face him,' she said determinedly. 'There's nothing he can do to us.'

'Oh, God!' he almost wept. 'You don't know what you're talking about. You don't know what he's like.'

When she didn't answer Toni stared at her, wild-eyed, and, with a sudden spurt of determination, grabbed the wheel. She slowed, trying to push him away and keep a straight course, but Toni was fighting her now, desperately trying to wrench the wheel aside.

The car slewed violently across the road and went into a spin. Donna struggled to recover control, crying out to Toni to release the wheel, but his hands were clamped on it in a frenzy and she couldn't get them off.

'*Toni!*' she screamed. '*Toni, please—*'

It was too late. The world was beginning to whirl about her as the car rose in the air and turned over and over.

That was the last thing Donna saw. But she heard everything: the screech of tyres, the crash as they landed, Toni crying her name again and again, until his voice faded away into silence.

Through her pain and anguish she understood the meaning of that silence. She whispered Toni's name, but she knew he couldn't hear her. He would never hear her again.

She was lost in red-hot darkness. It swirled around her, jabbing her body with knives, making every breath an agony. At last she opened her eyes. It took time for them to focus, but then she made out that she was in a small white room. The walls were white, and the ceiling, and the bed in which she lay.

There was a dark shadow beside the bed. Slowly she turned her head, and saw Rinaldo Mantini. His eyes were fixed on her, and her heart almost failed her, for never before had she seen a look of such total hatred on any human face.

CHAPTER FOUR

FOR a long moment they looked at each other, until at last Donna whispered, 'My baby?'

'Your child is safe,' Rinaldo told her in a distant voice. 'You were lucky.'

'And Toni?'

'My brother is dead,' Rinaldo said flatly.

'Oh, God!' she whispered in horror. In her heart she'd known it. The fading of Toni's voice in her delirium had had a final quality that told her the truth, but it was still terrible to hear it confirmed.

'How long have I been here?' she asked huskily.

'Two days. At first the doctors thought that the shock would kill you too. But you lived.'

'And you wish I was dead, don't you?' she asked, frightened by something cold and bleak in his face.

His expression didn't change. 'I'll tell the doctor you're awake,' he said, rising. 'We'll talk later.'

He disappeared. Nurses came. Donna drifted back into sleep. Her whole body ached and her heart was sick with misery, but she clung to the thought that her child was still alive.

She drifted in and out of consciousness for several days. Rinaldo was always there, watching her, his eyes unyielding. Through her troubled dreams she could feel the force of his hate. At last she woke, clear-headed for the first time. And he was still there.

'I didn't imagine it, did I?' she asked. 'You told me Toni is dead.'

'Dead,' he confirmed in a flat voice. 'His funeral was yesterday.'

She began to weep. 'Oh, God! Poor Toni!'

'Yes, weep for him,' Rinaldo said in a voice that was almost a sneer. 'Weep for the man you killed, but expect no pity from me.'

'I didn't kill Toni,' she protested weakly. 'It was an accident.'

'Yes, an accident caused by your greed,' he told her. 'Your determination to seize all you could and escape as fast as possible.'

'No—no—I was coming back to the Villa Mantini— Toni didn't want to return—he tried to stop me—'

'Don't make it worse by lying.'

'I'm not—'

'You took the money I offered you, and my grandfather's ring, and persuaded Toni to escape at night. Did you give one thought to what you were doing to those he loved? When Toni's grandfather heard of his death he collapsed. He was brought to this hospital with a stroke, and has lain at death's door ever since.'

'*No!*' Donna gave a scream of protest. So much death and misery was more than she could bear right now. She turned away from Rinaldo and buried her face in the pillow, shaking with anguish.

The noise brought a nurse hurrying into the room. 'Please, *signore*, the patient must not be agitated,' she said urgently.

'Never fear!' Donna heard Rinaldo's voice. 'This one has no heart. She causes destruction wherever she goes, but she escapes unharmed.'

The impact of the crash had knocked Donna unconscious, broken her ankle and two of her ribs, but mir-

aculously her child was unharmed. She soon began to
notice her surroundings, and to realise that she was in
a luxurious private ward. A middle-aged nurse, called
Alicia, seemed to be assigned exclusively to her care.
When she asked questions Alicia said, 'Signor Rinaldo
said you were to be brought here at his expense.'

'How kind of him,' Donna murmured.

'He's a very generous man,' Alicia confirmed. 'He's
a patron of this hospital, and has made it many gifts.'

But Donna knew that kindness had nothing to do with
Rinaldo's apparent concern for her. He'd had her
brought to a place where he could give orders. Alicia's
next words confirmed it.

'The police wish to speak to you about the accident
when you are well enough to talk,' she said. 'But they've
been told that won't be for some time. Don't worry. No
one will get in here to trouble you.'

She said it as reassurance, but it made Donna understand that she was a prisoner—Rinaldo Mantini's
prisoner, to be kept apart until he'd decided what to do
with her. She shivered.

She disliked the feeling of helplessness. The time had
come to see if she could walk, and when the nurse had
left she threw back the covers and gingerly set her un-
damaged foot on the ground. Her broken ankle was in
plaster, but by holding onto the end of the bed she
managed to rise slowly. When she was standing she
paused and took a deep breath.

She began to put one foot in front of the other. Her
legs were shaky but they supported her for a short way.
There was a small mirror on the wall, and she managed
to get close enough to see what had happened to her.

She looked dreadful, she thought. Her face was pale
and two livid bruises marked it. She gave herself a wry

smile and began to turn back, but suddenly her head started to swim and a feeling of nausea attacked her. She stretched out her arms, groping wildly for some support, but there was only empty air. Just as she was on the point of collapse she heard the door open, a harsh voice muttering a curse, and the next moment a man's hands seized her.

'What the devil do you think you're doing?' Rinaldo demanded.

'I just wanted—' She broke off and gasped as sickness swept over her. Without realising what she was doing she rested her head against his shoulder, glad only for the strength she found in him. He put his arm about her, careful of her damaged ribs, and supported her back to the bed. There he laid her down and drew the covers over her. 'I'm calling the nurse,' he said, grim-faced.

'No, I'm all right,' she gasped. 'There's some glucose by the bed. If I could just—'

He raised her with an arm under her shoulders and held the glass to her lips while she sipped. When she'd finished he laid her back. His movements had been gentle, but there was no gentleness in his face as he spoke.

'I forbid you to do such a thing again,' he said. 'If you can't be sensible I'll have a nurse posted in here all the time to keep an eye on you.'

'What does it matter to you what I do?' she demanded rebelliously.

'You're carrying my brother's child—or so you would have me believe.'

'But you *don't* believe it, do you? So why not just let me go?'

'When I'm sure about you, then I'll know what to do.'

The words had an ominous ring. Donna lay back tiredly against the pillows. Although he'd ministered to her needs there was nothing yielding about Rinaldo. He was doing what needed to be done, until he was 'sure about' her. It was suddenly very clear to Donna why Toni had had to escape his brother's shadow.

'When are you going to let the police talk to me?' she asked.

'When I've talked to you myself. Although, God knows, it's hardly necessary. The truth is plain enough.'

'And what do you think the truth is?'

'I offered you money to give Toni up, but you got greedy. You persuaded him to leave with you that night, and you took the money with you, also Piero's ring.'

'It's not true,' she said desperately. 'I left the money and the ring behind. Toni took them. I didn't find out until we stopped for petrol. I was furious with him. I said we must come back. I was looking forward to throwing your filthy money back at you.'

'Oh, please!' he said contemptuously. 'Surely you can do better than that! The car was found facing north. You were going away from Rome, not towards it. You must have been driving very fast to have such an accident.'

Her head swam, but she fought for the strength to speak calmly. 'I'm telling you the truth. I started to drive back to the villa. Toni tried to change my mind. When I wouldn't budge he grabbed the wheel. That was what made the car skid out of control. I know we went into the air and turned over...' She stopped, shuddering at the visions that fleeted through her head. 'That must have been...how the car...came to be facing the other way...'

'A very neat story to put the blame on Toni,' he grated.

'Surely someone must have seen what happened?'

'There were no witnesses. The road was empty but for you. How could you have an accident on a straight, empty stretch of road?'

'I've told you—Toni—'

'Ah, yes! How convenient for you that he's not here to defend himself. Why should he be so anxious not to come back?'

Donna leaned back against the pillows. Her strength was almost at an end, but she wouldn't let this man intimidate her. 'Perhaps he'd had enough of you steam-rollering over him,' she said quietly. 'Look into your own heart, Rinaldo, and ask yourself why he was so desperate not to face you again.'

Rinaldo's face was livid. If he'd been her enemy before, he was doubly so now. After a long moment he left the room.

She slept, woke, slept again. When she next opened her eyes it was morning. When she'd washed and eaten something Rinaldo appeared.

'I can't hold the police off any longer,' he said coolly. 'They'll be here in a minute. I must know what you're going to say to them.'

'The truth.'

His mouth twisted. 'You mean you're going to stick to your story.'

'I'm going to tell the truth,' she said wearily. A moment ago she'd been feeling strong, but suddenly the weakness had started to creep over her again. It was the effect of this domineering man's presence. Nothing and nobody could stand up to him, but somehow she must try.

Ten minutes later a young policeman was shown in.

'The *signorina* is still very unwell,' Rinaldo said. 'I hope this won't take long.'

'I only wish for a simple description of the facts, *signore*,' said the policeman. Despite his uniform he spoke with a hint of deference, as everybody did to Rinaldo.

He turned back to Donna. 'Who was driving the car?'

'I was.'

The young man's face became grave. 'Where were you heading for?'

'I was going towards Rome and the Villa Mantini,' she said firmly.

He frowned. 'We found the car facing the other way.'

'So I've been told.'

'And I believe you had left the villa not long before.'

'We left it in the early morning and drove for an hour. We stopped at a service station and decided to return. At least—I wanted to return. Toni disagreed, but I was in the driver's seat. I headed back the way we'd come and he—he yanked at the wheel to stop me. The car swerved and—' She closed her eyes.

'Why did you turn back so soon after your departure, *signorina*?'

'I discovered that I'd brought something with me that I hadn't meant to bring. I wanted to return it before continuing the journey,' she said, choosing her words carefully.

'And Signor Mantini did not agree with this?'

'No, he wanted to keep travelling. We had an argument and—and he pulled at the wheel.'

'So you maintain,' the policeman said in an expressionless voice, 'that the accident was the fault of Signor Antonio Mantini.'

She sighed. 'Yes, I do.' It felt dreadful to be blaming poor Toni, who was dead, but she had no choice.

'It's a pity he can't be here to confirm your statement,' the policeman murmured, and she could sense his disapproval. 'I'll have this prepared for you to sign.'

Rinaldo ushered him out. After a few minutes he returned, closing the door firmly behind him.

'So now you've saved yourself at the expense of my brother,' he said with contempt. 'Are you pleased with yourself?'

'I didn't lie,' she pleaded. 'Why can't you believe me?'

'Why should I? Can you imagine how you look to me? A few days ago all was well in my world. Then you arrived, with your greed, your deceit, your ruthless determination to mow down all who got in your way. And now my grandfather is near death, and my brother lies cold in the earth. Because of *you*.'

'Stop it!' she cried, burying her face in her hands.

'Does the truth hurt?' he sneered. 'Well, you'll just have to live with it.'

'And you?' she said, forcing herself to face him. 'What's the truth that *you're* afraid to face, Rinaldo?'

'The truth holds no terrors for me.'

'Doesn't it? Do you dare to admit that Toni was afraid of you? That's why he didn't want to come back.'

'That's enough,' he snapped. 'You know nothing, *nothing*. Isn't it enough that you blackened my brother's name to the police, without trying to blacken it to me too?'

'But perhaps it's not *his* name that the truth blackens,' she said defiantly. 'Why are you so afraid to look at yourself?'

He turned dreadful eyes on her. 'Don't make me hate you more than I already do.'

'I think you hate very easily. It's love you know nothing about. I loved Toni, or I wouldn't be having his child. I made him happy. He wanted to be with me. He ran away from you, towards me. That's the true reason why you hate me.'

He didn't answer in words, but he brought his fist down on a small cabinet. His whole body was trembling with the force of his emotion. When he lifted his head Donna saw that his face was ravaged. 'Stop tormenting me,' he said hoarsely. 'Why did you ever come into our lives?'

'Because Toni wanted me,' she cried.

'And you wanted what he had to give.'

'Yes,' she said boldly. 'I wanted what he had to give—love and tenderness. When he knew I was going to have his child he made me feel like a queen, and no one had ever made me feel like that before. But if I'd known about *you*, Rinaldo, I'd never have come near you. The sooner I'm away from here the better, and I hope I never have to see you again.'

'That's easily arranged,' he said, very pale.

'Let me see your grandfather, just once—'

'Never!' The word was like a whiplash.

'Then I'll have to go without seeing him. And you can forget I exist.'

'If only I could,' he said bitterly. 'But there's an empty place in my home, a place that will never be filled because of you.'

'I'm sorry,' she said in a softer voice. Even through her dislike of him she could sense that his anguish was real. 'But it's no use talking. You'll always think the worst of me. You'll find it easier when I'm out of your sight.'

'And your child? This baby that I'm supposed to believe is Toni's?'

'Forget me. Forget the baby. It's better that way. Also—I want you to take this.'

She pulled out her bag from the bedside table. Inside it were the possessions that had been retrieved from the accident, including the envelope containing the money and the ring.

'I found that I still had this,' she said. 'I thought you would have taken it.'

'While you were unconscious?' he said bitterly. 'I'm not a sneak thief. I wouldn't go rummaging through the possessions of a sick woman. Besides, I wanted the satisfaction of taking it back before your eyes.'

'Then you can do so now.' She held it out to him. 'Please take it. I want nothing from you.'

'How will you support your child?'

'That doesn't concern you.'

'Answer me,' he said angrily.

'I'm a nurse. I can always earn a living.'

'And who'll care for your baby while you do? Childminders? Babysitters drawn from God knows where because you have to hire the cheapest?'

She looked at him steadily. 'You've said that my child isn't Toni's. Why should you care what happens?'

He snatched the envelope from her and hurled it to the floor. 'Admit it,' he said, seizing her shoulders. 'Say that this isn't Toni's baby and I'll see you have enough to live on. *But for God's sake, admit it!*'

She knew a strange stirring of pity for him. He didn't know what to believe, except that, whatever the truth, he was faced with pain and misery. But her anger too was roused, and she refused to yield to softer feelings.

'I want nothing from you,' she said huskily. 'Can't you understand that?'

'Admit it! Say it isn't Toni's baby, and you can have anything you want.' His face was tortured.

'The only thing I want is to be free of you,' she cried. 'My child was fathered by Toni but it will carry *my* name, not his, because I'm finished with the Mantini family. I'll leave here as soon as I can, and I never want to see or hear from you again. Now please leave. I'm tired and I want to be alone.'

He stared at her for a moment. Then he walked out.

It was late at night, and Rinaldo was sitting in the garden, staring at the moonlight glittering on the fountain, when the maid came to tell him that a police officer had called. She had to speak to him twice before he came out of his unhappy dream. He pulled himself together and told her to show the man in. The officer was Gino Forselli, a man of Rinaldo's age whose rank proclaimed him far beyond making this kind of call. But the two men had been at school together, and greeted each other cordially.

'It was good of you to come yourself, Gino,' Rinaldo said, speaking with an effort, as though it had been a struggle to return to the world.

'I'm sorry to call so late, but I thought you'd be glad to hear the news.'

'About what?'

'A witness has come forward who saw the accident.'

Rinaldo slammed down his glass with an exclamation of triumph. 'At last! Now the truth will come out. No more lies! Why hasn't this witness spoken up before?'

'He was afraid to. He'd been visiting a lady in her husband's absence.'

Rinaldo grunted.

'He slipped out at dawn and was walking along the road when he saw a red, open-topped car approach. Everything in his statement confirms Signorina Easton's story. He says the car was travelling south, towards Rome—'

'What?' Rinaldo's voice was full of incredulity. He stared at Forselli, tense with baffled rage. 'Are you sure?'

'Completely. According to him the driver was a woman, with a man beside her. He saw the man grab the wheel, then the car began to slew across the road until the movements became so violent that it spun into the air, overturned twice and came to rest facing in the opposite direction. He ran back to his lady friend, called the police on her phone, and vanished.

'I must admit, I thought Signorina Easton's story sounded highly unlikely. After all, why should Toni seize the wheel like that? It would mean—'

'Never mind,' Rinaldo said harshly.

Gino Forselli coughed and added cautiously, 'There'll be no charges. Since I understand that this woman is— shall we say—close to your family, I wanted to be the first to tell you the good news.'

'Yes,' Rinaldo said heavily. 'Good news.'

Donna worried constantly about Piero. He alone had smiled and welcomed her, and she had brought him grief. Nurse Alicia said that Piero was 'as well as can be expected'. But she refused to reveal any more, and Donna had the feeling she was obeying Rinaldo's instructions.

She had better luck with her night nurse, Bianca, who had a chatty disposition, and let slip that Piero was at the far end of the building, on the next floor up. Donna didn't allow her interest to show in her face, but at dawn she slipped out of her ward and made her way towards the stairs that led up to the next floor.

She passed down corridor after corridor, studying the names on each door, her heart thumping with apprehension. She wasn't sure what would happen when she found Piero. She only knew that she must tell the kindly old man how sorry she was.

At last she reached a door bearing the card 'Signor Piero Mantini'. Now she was here her nerve nearly failed her, but she pulled herself together and softly turned the handle.

The room was almost dark, but she could just make out Piero's frail figure on the bed. He was lying with his eyes closed, pain and weariness written on his face. Tears stung her eyes as she remembered him as she'd last seen him, full of life and jollity. Now he looked as if the will to live had gone, and she had helped to do this to him.

Suddenly Donna felt that she'd done a terrible thing in intruding on him. Why should he want to see her? She turned and almost collided head on with Rinaldo. She gasped, for she hadn't seen him.

'What the devil are you doing here?' he snapped. 'Is nowhere safe from you?'

'I wanted to tell him how sorry I am,' she said desperately.

'And will your crocodile tears make any difference?'

'My feeling for him is real,' she insisted in a low, hurried voice. 'And if—if he understood that, it might ease his pain.'

'You don't know what you're talking about. Get out before I throw you out.'

There was a faint movement from the bed. Rinaldo swiftly went to Piero's side. 'It's all right, Nonno,' he said in a voice whose gentleness fell strangely on Donna's ears after the harsh way he'd spoken to her. 'Everything's all right. I'm here.'

Piero was trying to say something, but Donna could see that the stroke had left him paralysed. She looked at him in helpless pity, and began to back out of the room. But he saw her and all at once he was transfixed. His mouth contorted and frantic, frustrated sounds emerged from it. At first she thought he was distressed, but then she saw that he was fighting to raise an arm from the bed, reaching out to her.

Ignoring Rinaldo's displeasure, she went forward and gathered his hand between hers, smiling at him in reassurance. 'I've been worried about you,' she said softly. 'When they told me you were ill I had to come and see you—'

Tears threatened her. She fought them back and continued in a choking voice, 'I know how much you loved Toni. I loved him too.' She spoke without deception. At this moment her feelings for the dead boy came rushing back, and the final moments, when she'd turned against him, were forgotten. 'I wish it could all have been different,' she said huskily. 'I wish you hadn't had to be hurt—I wish—' She couldn't go on.

Piero answered, not with his mouth but with his eyes, which softened and told her that he didn't hate her. After the verbal battering she'd suffered from Rinaldo, Piero's gentle forgiveness was balm to her soul.

'You should go now,' Rinaldo said, speaking quietly but with an inflexible hardness in his voice. 'My grandfather is tired.'

'But he's trying to say something,' Donna said. She hadn't taken her eyes off Piero's face.

With a terrible effort he fought to speak but only the vague shapes of words emerged. Donna thought she made out the sound of 'baby'.

'The baby's fine,' she said, and knew by the glow in the old man's eyes that she'd said the right thing. Inspired, she placed his hand over her stomach. 'Still there,' she said. 'It would take more than an accident to finish off your great-grandchild.'

She felt Rinaldo stiffen beside her. She knew the words 'your great-grandchild' were provocative but she didn't care. She was speaking the truth.

Piero's eyelids drooped and the brightness died out of his face, leaving his skin grey. Donna felt Rinaldo's touch on her arm and looked up to find him indicating the door with his head. Impulsively she leaned down and kissed Piero's cheek before following Rinaldo out of the room. Outside the door she turned to face him, expecting condemnation. But his expression was blank and unreadable.

'Come with me,' he said.

When they were back in her own room Rinaldo said quietly, 'I don't understand anything about you. My grandfather was like a dead man. Then you appear, the woman who injured him, and suddenly he returns to life. It makes no sense.'

'It does to me,' Donna said. 'He has a loving heart. He isn't filled with bitterness as you are, Rinaldo. And I'm carrying Toni's child. He knows that, even if you don't, and it calls him back to life.'

She turned away, trying to escape the sensation of being overpowered that she had whenever she was near him.

'And when you've gone?' Rinaldo demanded. 'What will call him back to life then?'

'You'll have to do that.'

'I have no power to do so,' he said sombrely. 'It was always Toni with him.'

'I'll bring the baby to show him, if you'll let me. I know you think I'm lying, but I swear—' She stopped, for he had put up a hand.

'I had a call from the police last night,' he said. 'There was a witness to your accident.'

'And?' she asked tensely.

'I didn't believe you were telling the truth. Now it seems that I must. He confirms that you were driving back to Rome, and also—the other things you said.'

Donna sat down on the bed. The suddenness of the news had knocked her off balance. After a moment she looked up at Rinaldo, and found no softening in his expression. A rigid sense of honour had forced him to admit what he knew, but his hostility to her was unabated.

'So there's nothing to stop me going,' she said.

'There's everything to stop you going,' he said harshly. 'You're carrying my brother's child. I suppose I have to accept that now.'

'Because you've discovered that I was telling the truth about the accident?' she asked angrily. 'There's no connection.'

But there was a connection, and they both knew it. His picture of her as devious and deceitful had taken a knock, and he was no longer so convinced of his own judgement. She should have felt a sense of triumph. Instead she longed to get away from him, back to the safety of her own country. Once she'd dreamed of coming to Italy, but its stormy passions had defeated her. Now she only wanted to escape.

'I'm glad you believe me,' she said. 'But it makes no real difference.'

He stared at her. 'Of course it makes a difference. Do you think I'll allow my brother's child—perhaps his son—to be born out of wedlock? Such a thing is unthinkable; a dishonour.'

'Toni is dead. I can't marry him.'

'Of course not,' he said coldly. 'It is necessary that you marry me.'

She stared at him in outrage. 'If that's a joke, it's the unfunniest joke I've ever heard.'

He looked at her as though she'd said something in a foreign language. 'I do not make jokes,' he said flatly.

'Then you must be mad.'

'I was never more sane. It's the only possible solution.'

'Oh, no, it isn't! I've told you, I'm going back to England.'

His face tightened and she thought he would argue, but instead he relaxed again and merely said, 'In your present condition? How do you expect to travel?'

'Not now, but in a few days—'

'Very well. In a few days we'll discuss the matter again. I advise you to give my suggestion serious consideration.'

'Was it a suggestion?' she asked ironically. 'It sounded more of a diktat to me.'

'Well, I can't force you, can I?' he replied smoothly. 'I can only suggest and ask you to consider. Once we're married your child will be born legitimate. Your own life will be comfortable. Why should you refuse?'

'Why?' she echoed, scandalised. 'Because you've been my enemy from the first moment. Because there could never be peace between us. Because I dislike you intensely.'

He shrugged. 'I too have no liking for you. This is a matter of propriety. I don't wish Toni's child to be born a bastard. This is Italy, *signorina*. Such things matter here.'

'But I shan't be here,' she reminded him firmly.

He sighed impatiently. 'Very well, let's drop the subject. But don't be in too much of a hurry to leave. Your visit did my grandfather some good. Perhaps if you return often he'll start to improve. You owe him that.'

'Yes, I do,' she agreed instantly. 'I'm happy to do anything I can for him. He was so kind to me.'

'Good. I'll leave now, but I'll return later.'

He departed, leaving Donna's head aching. The discovery of Piero's condition, his warm response to her through the devastation of his illness, the knowledge that a witness to the accident had cleared her, and finally Rinaldo's shattering, outrageous proposal—all these had left her too shaken to think.

The worst of all was the suggestion that she should marry her enemy. For he was still her enemy. He'd made no bones about that. And her own hostility to him was so sharp that it pervaded her whole being. Marriage to a man she hated? No! Not for anything in the world.

But her indignation was pierced by a treacherous memory that returned insistently, despite her attempts to shut it out. That first night, they'd sat together by the fountain and he'd told her that she would never belong to Toni.

'You've known it from the moment we met.'

He'd touched her face with his fingertips, sending flickers of fire through her body, murmuring words she'd feared yet longed to hear.

'You're not a girl but a woman. You need a man.'

'Not you,' she'd protested.

But it could have been him. This was the man who might have brought her heart and body to life. If only things had been different...

She gave herself a shake and came back to reality. It was too late. It had been too late even before they met. Now they were foes, and the brief, treacherous attraction was consigned to the limbo of might-have-been. She belonged to Toni, who had loved her in his own way, and whose death lay on her conscience more than she would admit to Rinaldo.

It was he who'd caused the accident, but perhaps if she'd handled the situation better he might not have panicked. Or if she'd never come into his life at all he would be alive now. That was the burden she carried. And the weight of it would crush her again whenever she looked at Toni's brother.

CHAPTER FIVE

Soon after breakfast Alicia came in with a wheelchair. 'I've come to move you,' she said. 'You've been assigned a different ward, next to Signor Piero.'

Donna didn't have to ask who'd ordered that. It made perfect sense, but Rinaldo's high-handedness annoyed her. She seethed in silence as she collected her things and let Alicia settle her into the wheelchair.

Her new room was pleasant, especially when her possessions had been delivered. Donna immediately limped next door. Evidently the nurse had been warned to expect her arrival, for she ushered her in with a smile. It seemed that any arrangement made by Rinaldo went smoothly.

Piero was lying asleep. Donna sat quietly by the bed, and stayed without moving. 'How bad is he?' she asked the nurse.

'At first we thought he would die, but he's held on. I think he'll live, but it will only be a half life. He's mostly paralysed, and he can't speak except to make a few sounds.'

Once he opened his eyes and smiled at Donna, but he went back to sleep straight away, and she returned next door.

In the evening Rinaldo visited his grandfather, then came to see her. 'Is this to your liking?' he asked, looking at her surroundings.

'It's a nice room, but it would have been more to my liking if you'd mentioned it to me first, instead of just having me fetched like a parcel.'

'It didn't occur to me that you would object.'

'I only object to not having been consulted. And what about the person who was already in here?'

'I assure you it was very easily fixed.'

'You mean you gave your orders and everyone jumped,' she said crossly.

'That's usually how I manage my affairs,' he replied, with a touch of surprise. 'Why not?'

'Why not indeed? But not me. I'll do all I can for Piero, because I like him. But as soon as I'm well enough I'm going.'

He gave a slight shrug. 'Have I said otherwise?'

'As long as we understand each other.'

'How are you feeling?'

'I'm improving very fast, thank you.'

'And the baby?'

'The baby is doing well.'

'Take good care of him.'

That made her very angry. 'Do you think I need you to tell me to care for my own child?'

'But it's not only yours, is it?'

'Legally it is.'

'You mean to shut Toni's family out completely?' he asked in a voice that might almost have been indifferent.

'Let's just say I won't let you interfere. I thought I'd already made that plain.'

'Yes,' he said. 'You did. Very plain. But I hope your dislike of me won't make you leave hospital too soon. You should remain here for another couple of weeks, for your child's sake.' His voice was coolly ironical. 'Am I allowed to suggest that, or am I being unbearably high-handed?'

'This is a private hospital, isn't it? I don't like the fact that the expense falls on you.'

'I do it for Toni. Can't you find it in your heart to allow me that?'

'If you put it that way, I have no choice.'

'You are all graciousness. And if the expense worries you repay me by caring for Piero.' A wintry look came over his face. 'Your company does him more good than mine. I'll trouble you as little as possible.'

Slightly to her surprise, he kept his word over the next fortnight. He visited Piero each day. If Donna was there she would slip away to leave them alone. He would look in for five minutes before his departure, and enquire politely after her health. His manner was coolly civil, and he uttered no barbed words.

Once, while Donna was sitting with Piero, holding his hand and talking to him gently, she looked up to find Rinaldo regarding her with a dark expression. He'd entered the room unheard. Now she'd caught him off guard. Unhappiness shadowed his face, but for once there was no anger there, and when he realised that she was looking at him he took a deep breath and seemed to come out of a dream.

'Is he any better?' he asked her.

'He's getting stronger every day. He still can't talk, or move very much, but he speaks to me with his eyes.' She rose from her seat. 'I'll leave you now.'

'There's no need.'

'No, you'll want to be alone with him,' she said, slipping quickly out of the room.

That was how it was between them—restrained courtesy, not meeting each other's eyes, except by accident, as though each was secretly afraid of what they would find there. In this way the time slipped away peacefully. The only agitation was Donna's discovery that she couldn't find her passport, but this soon reappeared, having been mislaid during the move, and later found in a locker.

With a shock she realised that over three weeks had passed. Soon she must move on, and the thought that troubled her most was how to tell Piero. He was almost well enough to go home. Rinaldo had briefly informed her that the preparations were in train—his room had been adapted for a disabled man, and the nurses engaged. And on the day he left the hospital she would say goodbye to him.

She tried to prepare his mind one day. 'We won't be able to talk like this much longer,' she said gently. 'You'll be going home in a few days and—well, everything is going to change.'

He smiled. Donna took a deep breath. This was going to be harder than she'd expected.

'It will be different for me too,' she said cautiously. 'You see—' She stopped as she became aware that Piero was trying to move his hand. At last he managed to point to Donna's left hand. With dismay she realised that he was indicating her wedding finger. Indistinct sounds came from him as he struggled to enunciate a word.

'M-m-moglie—' he managed at last.

She was astounded. *Moglie* was the Italian word for wife, but she wasn't going to be a wife. Could Piero's mind be wandering? Had he not, after all, realised that Toni was dead?

'Piero,' she said gently, 'I can't be Toni's wife...'

'R-Rinaldo—' he managed.

She stared at him as some glimmer of the dreadful truth got through to her. But her mind refused to accept it. Surely even Rinaldo wouldn't dare do such a dictatorial, outrageous thing?

But the question answered itself. Of course he would dare. Why not? He was used to getting his own way, simply riding over the opposition if necessary. Her refusal had been merely a temporary inconvenience.

Her anger was so overpowering that she knew she must get out at once. Piero mustn't be upset.

'I'll—be back soon,' she said, and left quickly.

Once in her own room she sat on the edge of the bed, shivering with her inner turmoil. It wasn't just anger that consumed her, but a kind of shocked awe at the lengths to which Rinaldo was prepared to go. For the last few weeks he'd let her think he'd forgotten his incredible proposal, and all the time he'd been making plans to brush her opposition aside as something of no importance.

Someone was coming along the corridor and going into Piero's room. After a while Rinaldo entered her room, closed the door behind him, and stood looking at her.

Donna returned his gaze.

'I didn't misunderstand, did I?' she snapped. 'Piero is expecting us to marry. You've been arranging a wedding all this time, even after I made it clear that I'd have nothing to do with it?'

'I have.'

'Is that all you can say?'

'There is nothing else to say. I hadn't planned for you to find out like this. I didn't know Piero could communicate enough to tell you.'

'I wonder when you did plan to tell me?' she demanded indignantly. 'Halfway to the church?'

'Look, I understand that you're annoyed—'

'I hope you understand my annoyance rather better than you understood my refusal. Has nobody ever said no to you before, Rinaldo? Is that why you don't recognise the word?'

'I was sure you'd come to your senses when your health had improved. It was sensible to set things in train. So I did.'

'Including telling your grandfather? That was utterly unscrupulous.'

'It's given him something to live for. It would break his heart if I let you leave.'

'What do you mean, "let" me leave? I don't need your permission. I shall just go.'

'That I will not allow,' he said simply.

'*You* won't—? Who are you to allow me or not allow me? I don't take your orders.'

His dark eyes flashed and for a moment she saw a glimpse of the imperial authority that had once made Rome great. 'Donna, it's time we understood each other. I'm not asking you for your consent to this marriage. I'm telling you that neither of us has any choice. This is something we have to do—'

'I don't have to do it,' she said desperately. 'There's always a choice—'

'Very well, then,' he said impatiently. 'It was my decision and I've made it for the honour of my family and the welfare of my brother's child. You cannot refuse.'

'Try me.'

'Toni wouldn't want you to refuse. He loved you. He'd want you and his child to be safe.'

She drew a swift, painful breath. 'How could you sink so low as to use Toni as a weapon?'

'I'm not using him as a weapon,' he said harshly. 'I'm reminding you of your obligation to him. He'd be glad that I'm going to protect his family. In this country family counts for a lot.'

Donna turned away, covering her ears with her hands, trying to shut him out, but it was in vain. This man's power was hypnotic. He could make the most outrageous demands sound reasonable. There was no escape from him.

He moved swiftly, turning her towards him, pulling her hands down, forcing her to listen to him. 'Listen to me. The wedding is set for the day after tomorrow. There's no point in arguing.'

She stared at him in outraged disbelief. '*The day after*— How could even you arrange that? Aren't there formalities—?'

'Of course. But in view of your state of health the officials didn't insist on your being personally present. Your passport was enough.'

'My—*you stole my passport*?'

'Borrowed it, since I believe it has now been returned to you.'

'So that was why it disappeared. How dare you?'

'It was necessary,' he said impatiently. 'I couldn't make the arrangements without it.'

'Then you should have spared yourself the trouble. I'm leaving tomorrow, and that's the last you'll ever see of me.'

Instead of repeating his insistence Rinaldo studied his nails for a moment. When he lifted his head his face was unreadable. 'Perhaps you're right,' he said. 'It was foolish of me to think you would submit to force. I admired your spirit the night we met.'

She breathed a little more easily. 'I'm glad you understand.'

He gave her a strange look. 'You and I understood each other from the beginning, didn't we, Donna?'

'I—don't understand you.'

'Don't you? Was it all in my imagination, then?'

His eyes held hers, reminding her of things she would rather forget.

'Have you never wondered,' Rinaldo went on, 'what would have happened if we'd met some other way?'

She gave a little sigh. 'We'll never know. It doesn't matter now. There are too many barriers between us. I was Toni's woman.'

'But you wouldn't have been—if I'd met you first.'

Suddenly she saw the danger and backed away from it. This was another of his unscrupulous schemes. 'You're a clever man, Rinaldo,' she said. 'Luckily for me, I know how clever you are.'

He gave a wry laugh. 'I didn't take you in, did I?'

'Not for a minute. I know there are no lengths you wouldn't go to to get what you want.'

He shrugged. 'Well, I'd better tell my grandfather that the wedding is off.'

'Will he mind very much?'

He stopped at the door. 'Yes, he'll mind very much. But that's no longer any concern of yours.' He went out.

Donna stayed where she was, racked by feelings that pulled her in ten directions at once. She knew she'd done the right thing, but the thought of Piero's pain hurt her.

After a few minutes Rinaldo reappeared. 'He wants to see you.'

The old man gave a crooked smile as she entered. 'How did he take it?' Donna asked in a low voice so that Piero couldn't hear.

'I haven't told him,' Rinaldo said. 'You're going to tell him.'

She gasped and tried to pull away, but Rinaldo's hands were firm on her shoulders, blocking her escape. He'd outmanoeuvred her again.

'Say it,' Rinaldo repeated with soft vehemence. 'Break his heart. Tell him that the dream that's kept him alive is over.'

'How could you do this?' she breathed.

'Because our marriage *has* to take place. Haven't you understood that yet?'

He urged her to the bed. His grip was superficially light, but she could feel the steely strength in the arm about her shoulders. Donna took a deep breath. She must tell Piero the truth now, before another moment passed.

But the words died before the shining look in his eyes. She had done this to him, and she couldn't hurt him more.

Feebly Piero stretched out his good hand to her. She took it and dropped to her knees beside the bed. He was struggling to speak.

'*Figlia,*' he said at last, softly.

Despite her turmoil her heart leapt at the word. *Figlia.* Daughter. Not even granddaughter, but daughter. It was years since anyone had called her that. Suddenly she was shaken by sobs. She lifted the frail hand in her own and laid her cheek against it, wetting it with her tears. She knew she couldn't fight any longer. Rinaldo had trapped her, just as he'd always meant to.

'He's trying to say something else,' Rinaldo said.

Donna looked up and released Piero's hand so that he could point. He indicated her and then Rinaldo, and whispered, '*Bene.*' Good. Piero had given them his blessing.

His lips continued to move, and Donna thought he was repeating, '*Bene.*' Then she realised that he was saying another word that began with B. At last she made

it out, and to her horror realised that the word was
'*bacio*'. Kiss.

'What is he saying?' Rinaldo asked. 'I can't hear.'

'It's nothing,' she said hastily.

'Let me be the judge of that.'

Piero managed to raise his voice a little. '*Bacio,*' he
repeated huskily.

Donna rose and moved away from the bed, but
Rinaldo detained her with a hand on her arm. 'My
grandfather wants us to kiss,' he said.

'*No,*' she said, speaking quietly with her face averted.
'I couldn't. *I couldn't*. How can he ask such a thing
when he knows—?'

'You misunderstand. What Piero wants from us is a
kiss not of passion but of tenderness. He knows that
we're marrying for Toni's sake, but he needs to feel that
there can be peace between us.'

'Peace?' she whispered, looking at him out of stormy
eyes. 'Peace between us?'

'You're right,' he murmured. 'Such peace was never
meant to be. But we can pretend for his sake.'

She didn't try to resist as he drew her closer and placed
his fingers under her chin. 'Look up at me,' he
murmured.

Unwillingly she did so. His eyes were dark and they
seemed to draw her in. Rinaldo bent his head and laid
his lips gently against hers.

His mouth barely touched her, and yet she felt as if
a burning brand had seared her. She wanted to escape
from him, but she couldn't move. Her senses were reeling
from the feel of him. His lips were warm and firm. Once
again the thought would not be denied. This was a man,
not a boy. There was strength and purpose in the way

he held her, one hand on her shoulder, the other behind her head.

She should never have agreed to this kiss. Marriage to Rinaldo would only be tolerable if she could shut out all awareness of him as a man she might have loved, in another life. But how could she ignore such things when his lips were on hers and she could feel the power of his body against her own? Her pulse was racing, and her whole body seemed to be caught up in the hot, insistent rhythm.

If only he would stop, she thought wildly. But she didn't want him to stop. She wanted this kiss to go on for ever, thrilling her with the sweet, new sensations. They possessed her utterly, revealing depths of awareness within herself that she'd never dreamed of before. And it was all too late. Now, in the very moment that she'd agreed to marry him, she knew that the barriers would always be between them.

He released her. Donna looked up into his face and saw on it a dark look that she couldn't understand. Was he as shaken as herself? Or was he merely angry? Perhaps he'd sensed her reaction to him, and despised her for it. She pulled away from him, trying to get command of herself.

Piero was smiling contentedly. His lips shaped Rinaldo's name.

'Yes, Nonno,' Rinaldo said at once.

With his eyes Piero indicated the little table at his bedside, on which stood a tiny box. When Rinaldo opened it he discovered the emerald and ruby ring that Piero had given Donna the first night.

'He wants you to have this again,' Rinaldo said.

Donna nodded. She was beyond words. Rinaldo took her hand and spoke softly.

'There's no guard on the door, Donna. Despite what I've said, if you really refuse to marry me, no one will stop you leaving. Now is the time to say.'

'You know I can't,' she whispered.

He gripped her hand. 'Let me hear you say that you will marry me.'

'I'll marry you.'

He slipped the ring onto her finger, and she knew that now there was no turning back.

The next day—the day before the wedding—both she and Piero left hospital and returned to the Villa Mantini. Rinaldo had engaged two nurses to care for Piero, but Donna stayed with him until he was comfortably settled in his room. He seemed happier when she was there.

He was not to attend the wedding in the town hall. Normally this would be followed by a religious service, but Rinaldo had decreed that a civil ceremony would be enough, and Donna was glad. To have entered this incongruous marriage in church would have felt like sacrilege.

To her surprise Selina had insisted that the honour of attending the bride should fall to her.

'She does this as a gesture of friendship,' Rinaldo explained. 'It means a great deal to her.'

'What have you told her?' Donna asked.

Rinaldo looked surprised. 'The truth, of course. I couldn't hope to deceive her. She knows you were engaged to Toni.'

'What about the rest of the world?'

'The rest of the world won't dare to ask.'

'But surely they'll wonder?'

'At first. With luck, in time the details will fade and people will assume the child is mine.'

'Unless Selina entertains them with the truth,' Donna said a little sharply.

'I don't know why you've taken against her,' Rinaldo said, annoyed. 'She's a friend of mine and she wants to show you nothing but kindness.'

'But it isn't natural,' Donna protested. 'Toni told me she wanted to marry you herself.'

'Toni had to dramatise everything,' Rinaldo said impatiently. 'If Selina wanted to marry me she could have done so thirteen years ago.'

'But you *were* in love with her?'

'Madly, desperately,' Rinaldo said in an indifferent voice. 'In love as only a boy of twenty can be in love. She turned me down to take up a film part. She was perfectly right. Our marriage wouldn't have been a success. She said I was possessive—which I was. She wanted to follow her star. Those days are over. Now she's my friend, and I ask you to treat her civilly. Is that too much to ask?'

'Of course not,' Donna said. 'And after all—it's none of my business.'

'That's true,' Rinaldo said after a moment.

On the wedding day Selina arrived early, all smiles, and embraced Donna with every appearance of warmth. She insisted on doing her hair, and did it expertly. But the style was fussy and didn't suit her. Selina herself was dressed in cream silk and pearls, with a large hat. Her face was flawlessly made up, and radiant, as though she were the bride.

Enrico drove the three of them to the town hall. He was Maria's nephew, a big, cheerful man whom his aunt usually referred to as 'that idiot'. He did gardening, driving and odd jobs.

When they arrived Rinaldo went away to complete some formality. Donna and Selina were left awkwardly together. Donna caught a glimpse of herself in a mirror. As she'd suspected, the fussy hairdo was unbecoming.

'I wish I'd had more time to work on your appearance,' Selina sighed. 'You should have had a proper dress.'

'I appreciate all you've done,' Donna said, trying to be polite. 'But I'd rather everything was kept very simple. This isn't—quite like other weddings.'

'Of course. Rinaldo has explained everything to me. He marries you because he must. Otherwise he and I—' She broke off with a shrug. 'I'm a realist. And so— I hope—are you.'

'What do you mean?'

'Oh, come. We're both women of the world. Rinaldo is a man with a strong sense of duty and family honour. It makes him do what otherwise he wouldn't have dreamed of doing. After all, you're as indifferent to him as he is to you, but you're marrying him for the sake of your baby. I admire you for it.' She gave her a dazzling smile. 'I think you have the soul of a good mother. You know what they say. Some women are born to be wives, and some to be mothers.'

'And some to be mistresses?' Donna added lightly.

Selina beamed at her. 'I knew we'd understand each other. But then, you're much brighter than you look, aren't you?'

'I'm certainly brighter than you think I am,' Donna said firmly.

There was no more chance to talk, and no need for it, Donna realised. Everything had been communicated in those few minutes. Now all that was left was for her to walk to her meaningless wedding to a man who cared nothing for her, and try to come to terms with the shocking feelings that had destroyed her peace.

Donna moved through her wedding day in a dream, and afterwards could recall nothing clearly. At some time in her uneasy trance she and Rinaldo stood before civic officials and spoke the words that made them husband and wife in the eyes of the law. Donna thought of Toni, who should have been there with her. Would their marriage have stood any more or less of a chance of success than this strange, incredible union?

Throughout it all she was conscious of Selina, radiant in her beauty, a stark contrast to Donna's pallor and unease.

Then came the journey home in the car, with the three of them trying not to be self-conscious; Selina chattering away while the bride and groom avoided each other's eye.

At the Villa Mantini they went through the semblance of a marriage feast, but Donna escaped as soon as she decently could, using Piero as an excuse. She saw him settled for the night and stayed talking to him for a while. He indicated for her to return downstairs, but she shook her head.

'I'd rather stay with you,' she said simply.

She wondered what the other two were talking about. Was Rinaldo looking at Selina and contrasting her with his dull bride? Suddenly Donna was too tired to care. It had been a full day, and she was four months pregnant.

With a blinding sense of revelation it dawned on her that she had the answer to her stormy feelings. How many times had she advised newly expectant mothers about this very thing?

'There are so many hormone changes going on inside you just now,' she'd said to them, 'that it'll probably make you more emotional than usual. Don't worry about it. You'll settle down eventually.'

Of course. That was it. The sudden riot of her feelings really had nothing to do with Rinaldo. It was an illusion brought about by her pregnancy. To think that she'd been afraid that she might fall in love with him! And all the time it had simply been a clinical phase. The relief was so great that she nearly laughed out loud.

From down below she could hear noises. Looking out of the window, she saw Rinaldo's car, which Enrico had brought to the front door. Selina stepped inside, and Enrico drove her away. A few minutes later she heard Rinaldo mounting the stairs.

'I said goodbye to Selina for you,' he told her as he came into Piero's room.

'Thank you.' Donna kissed Piero. 'I'll go to bed now. I'm very tired.'

Rinaldo held the door open for her, and she returned to her bedroom. His own sleeping arrangements hadn't been mentioned between them, and it occurred to her how few things they had actually discussed. But one didn't discuss things with Rinaldo. One listened while he laid down the law. To her relief there was no sign of his things in her room.

Half an hour later there was a knock on her door, and Rinaldo's voice called, 'May I come in?'

She was in her dressing gown, and had pulled the elaborate hairdo down. 'Yes, come in,' she replied.

He too had undressed for bed. He was wearing a silk dressing gown over pyjamas whose open edges revealed the thick hairs on his chest. Donna felt a jolt of pleasure before she could suppress it. However much she disliked Rinaldo, he was an attractive male animal. She was glad that she'd remembered in time that the attraction wasn't real, but merely the result of her turbulent hormones.

'Are you all right?' he asked. 'The day hasn't tired you too much?'

'I'm perfectly well, thank you,' she said politely.

'Is there anything you need?'

'No, thank you.'

'Then I'll bid you goodnight.'

'Goodnight.'

She had a feeling that he wanted to say something else, but after hesitating for a few moments he went away.

CHAPTER SIX

DONNA was woken by the chiming of bells. She rose and went to the window, throwing open the shutters on a magical scene. Her view was over the countryside. Far away rose the seven hills of Rome. Nearby there were winding roads, and villages with little churches whose bell chimes were carried to her in the clear dawn air. A soft light lay over the countryside. Donna was silent, awed by so much beauty.

From here she could see the Mantini land. Close by the house, shaded by trees, lay some ground that had been separated from the rest by railings. This was the family burial plot. It was here that she would find Toni.

She dressed quickly, noticing that the clothes she'd worn before her spell in hospital were tighter. Before she left the room she took her little wedding posy from the vase where she'd placed it the night before.

It wasn't hard to find the plot. There were the headstones of Giorgio and Loretta Mantini, and a few others who appeared, from their dates, to be grandparents, aunts and uncles. And there, flat on the ground, was a square marble slab, newer than all the rest.

Beneath it lay all that remained of the vital boy who'd filled her life with love and laughter, however briefly. She no longer imagined herself in love with him, but she was torn with pity for his fate. Toni had been irresponsible, and weak. But he'd also been kind and generous in his careless fashion. He'd deserved better than this.

Donna held the posy against her face for a moment, and when she laid it on the tomb it was wet with her tears.

'I'm sorry,' she whispered. 'I'm so very sorry.'

She had an overwhelming awareness of another presence, and when she glanced up she saw Rinaldo, watching her. But he moved back into the shadows before she could speak, and when she next looked he was gone.

They met properly at breakfast. Rinaldo was there first, seated at the long table in the dining room. He rose and courteously pulled out a chair for her, opposite him.

'We won't usually eat together in the mornings,' he said. 'I leave for work very early, before the day becomes too hot. I'll be home at about eight o'clock in the evening, and we should be seen to dine together. You need have no fear of my troubling you at other times.'

She wasn't sure how to respond to this last remark, but Rinaldo didn't seem to need an answer. He was telling her how he'd arranged her life, and there was nothing for her to do but acquiesce.

'I have something here that requires your signature,' he said, pushing papers towards her. 'I've opened a bank account for you. The money will be available to you tomorrow.'

She stared when she saw the amount. 'I shan't need that much,' she protested.

'Nonsense, of course you will,' he said with a brusqueness that robbed the words of any amiability. '*My wife* is expected to dress well, and that takes money. Please don't argue about this.'

'Very well.'

'You'll also need to buy things for the baby. Just sign there, and then I must be going. You'll find a parcel in your room. It arrived from England this morning.'

He stuffed the signed papers into his briefcase, and departed. Donna had a light breakfast of coffee and rolls, then hurried upstairs, eager to investigate the parcel.

As she'd suspected, it came from a friend who had a key to the flat she'd recently shared with Toni. He'd gathered up some letters that had arrived there, and sent them on.

There were a couple of minor items for herself, and several credit card statements for Toni. The amounts gave her a shock. She'd always known that her lover was a spendthrift, but she hadn't imagined anything like this. His debts were at least three times what he'd admitted to her, and in addition there was a letter from the finance company about his car. Toni had fallen behind again with the repayments, and now the whole amount was due.

She couldn't think straight at the moment. She thrust everything back into the big envelope and went along the corridor to Piero's room. He was dressed, and sitting in a wheelchair by the window, Sasha purring on his lap. His weary face lit up at the sight of her. His love was the one bright spot in a lonely world, and it was going to have to be enough to help her endure the next few months.

She spent the morning with him. While she was eating a light lunch Maria told her what she was planning for the evening meal. Did the *patrona* approve?

'It sounds lovely,' Donna said.

'*Grazie, patrona.*'

Maria vanished at once, leaving Donna puzzled by the feeling that she'd wanted to escape. When she'd first come here she'd thought she had Maria's goodwill, but now the old woman seemed very anxious to get away from her. Did she too blame her, and regard her as a schemer?

Most of the afternoon was spent writing to her neighbour, and taking a nap. In the evening Rinaldo returned. When he'd visited Piero husband and wife dined formally together downstairs. He was polite, but nothing more. It was a relief when he asked her to excuse him, as he'd brought work home.

That first day set the pattern for the others that followed. Occasionally she would see Rinaldo at breakfast. More often she would hear his car leave early, and eat alone. She spent as much time as possible with Piero. His nurses were at first inclined to regard Donna as a well-meaning amateur. But when they learned of her professional qualifications and, more importantly, saw her with Piero they relaxed. Soon they were deferring to her.

She set herself to improve his condition, but the stroke had been a massive one, leaving him almost entirely paralysed. Sometimes he could force out the rough semblance of a word, but the effort tired him, and the odd word wasn't enough to put him in touch with the world. He was a man with a subtle brain and complex thoughts, and the frustration of not being able to communicate properly was terrible for him.

Donna read to him, talked to him, or just sat with him listening to the radio or watching television. To Donna's dismay, he showed no signs of regaining his abilities. He had stabilised but that was all. It seemed as if he faced a lifetime entombed in his own unresponsive body.

One evening she was sitting with him, listening to music and contentedly scratching Sasha's ears. It was late but Rinaldo was still not home, and soon she would go to bed. She looked at Piero, who was lying with his eyes closed, wondering if he'd gone to sleep. Then she noticed that the fingers of his left hand were softly beating time to the music.

The sight riveted her. Piero had been able to move his arm a little, but not individual fingers. But now the fingers were making clear, separate movements, and it gave her a flash of inspiration.

'Piero,' she said urgently. He opened his eyes. 'Look.' She took his hand and placed it in her own. 'Can you draw a letter—any letter?'

Instantly his eyes were alert. Slowly, with infinite concentration, he shaped a letter in her palm with the tip of his forefinger. It was a D.

'Another,' she said excitedly.

He shaped an O. Then, without waiting for her to urge him further, he drew an N, and another, and an A. Donna.

'You can talk,' she said, thrilled. 'You can say anything you want.'

He began to write in her hand again. When he reached the third letter she said, 'Yes, it will be slow. But we can *talk*. That's what matters.'

He began to draw again. *You're clever.*

'No, you're the clever one. Oh, I can't wait for Rinaldo to get home and hear about this.'

Let's talk now.

When Rinaldo returned an hour later he was astonished to hear laughter coming from his grandfather's room. He opened the door on a scene of merriment. Donna was sitting by the bed, raising a glass of orange juice. As Rinaldo watched she clinked it against the glass that Piero was just managing to hold, with her help.

'Here's to us!' she cried. 'We're brilliant.'

'What's happening?' Rinaldo asked.

Donna turned a smiling face on him. 'Piero can talk again,' she said. She removed Piero's glass, leaving his hand free. 'Watch.'

Slowly he spelt into her palm, *Thank you, my dear.*

Rinaldo stared for a moment, before raising his head and looking her directly in the eye. He seemed thunderstruck. When she stood back he took her place at the bed. Donna slipped out of the room and left them together.

It was late, and the concentration had tired her more than she'd realised. She went straight to her room and lay down, wondering if Rinaldo would come and talk to her. But soon her eyes closed, and she drifted off to sleep.

When Rinaldo left his grandfather's room he hesitated in the corridor. He knew how much Piero's new skill was due to Donna. Piero himself had told him so, and expressed his heartfelt relief that she'd stayed with them. *What would we do without her*? he'd asked. And Rinaldo had given a forced smile and said, 'I don't know.'

Now he felt he should see Donna, and thank her, but he was torn by conflicting feelings. It had been simpler in the days when he'd felt only hostility towards her, he reflected. But then disturbing memories came flooding back, and he knew that there'd never been a time when his feelings about her had been uncomplicated.

There was no answer to his tap on her door. He turned the handle and looked in. Donna was lying on the bed, still with the small table lamp on, as though she'd meant to stay awake, but couldn't manage it.

Rinaldo moved quietly to the windows and closed the shutters. Before turning off the lamp he stood for a moment looking down at her face. It was as soft and defenceless as a child's, and for a desperate moment he wished she would stay one thing or the other, so that he could know what to think about her. But that day might never come. He felt as if he could only see her through distorting filters, which constantly altered.

He switched off the light and left without waking her. Downstairs he wandered out into the grounds, to where the burial plot lay. Pain twisted inside him as he reflected that on the first day after their wedding she'd come to lay her wedding bouquet on his brother's grave. She'd come every day since, with fresh flowers plucked from Loretta's garden. This morning's offering lay there now, its white petals gleaming in the moonlight. He lifted one flower, holding it against his face, and it seemed to him that it was wet with her tears.

Donna spent the next day talking with Piero. Through his new method of communication he was able to tell her why he didn't blame her for the accident.

Toni—bad boy. Charming, lovable, but always in trouble. He said many things—not true—whatever was easiest. Why—crash?

Donna hesitated, unwilling to hurt him with the details, but he wrote in her hand, *Tell me.*

She related the story simply, and when she'd finished he gripped her hand.

I thought—something like that. Not your fault. He always ran away from difficulties.

'Yes, I began to realise,' she said sadly.

You must raise his child to be stronger. Rinaldo will help you. He's a strong man, a good man.

'And a very unforgiving one,' Donna mused. 'Why must he be so unyielding all the time?'

Because he doesn't dare to look into his own heart. You must help him. You loved Toni. Now you must love Rinaldo—not an easy man to love—but needs love very much.

Something stirred inside her. Would it be so very difficult to love Rinaldo? If she'd met him first, before Toni—

She wouldn't let herself think any more. What was the use? Rinaldo's attitude towards her was still mostly one of distrust and hostility. He'd learned to have some respect for her, but there was no softening in him.

He'd thanked her gravely for helping Piero find a way to 'speak'. 'It means everything to me to see him find some interest in life again,' he'd said the next day. 'You have all my gratitude.' But he'd been full of tension as he'd spoken.

Now that a method had been found, Donna sought other ways to make it easier for Piero. She bought a set of children's alphabet bricks, thinking that he might point to the letters he wanted. But Sasha, convinced that this was a new toy, kept pawing the bricks and confusing everyone. At last the idea was abandoned and Sasha was made a present of the whole set, whereupon she immediately lost interest.

Although Rinaldo loved his grandfather his nature was too impatient for him to sit while letters were spelled out one by one. His contribution was a word processor with a specially enlarged keyboard, upon which Piero could tap out letters. But the keyboard seemed to confuse him. Or perhaps he just preferred people to machines. So this idea too was abandoned, and he continued to write in Donna's palm.

One evening, about a month after their marriage, Donna sat preparing herself for dinner. That afternoon

Piero had repeated his insistence that Rinaldo needed
love. It was something he told Donna often, watching
her closely, as if trying to decide whether it was too soon
for her to love him. Despite the difficulties, the words
gave her a strange feeling of hope and expectancy. She
waited eagerly for his return.

But when he entered the house she knew at once that
something was wrong. There was an extra constraint in
his manner, and his eyes held an odd glitter. During the
meal she several times found him regarding her cynically.

'Is something the matter?' she asked at last.

'Yes. I thought we could wait until later, but since you
ask I want explanations from you, and they have to be
good.'

The glitter in his eyes had grown more pronounced.
There was no doubt of it. This was a man in a furious
temper.

'I don't know what I have to explain,' she said.

'Indeed? Well, let's start with the dress you're wearing.
It's been cleverly let out, but you never bought it in Italy.
In fact I recognise it from our very first meeting. And
I'd like to know why you're altering clothes when I gave
you money to buy new ones.'

'I—it seemed a waste to buy new clothes before I get
much bigger,' she stammered.

'For God's sake!' he exclaimed in disgust. 'Why don't
you tell me the truth? You've been sending money to
England. I only found out today. Practically every penny
I gave you has been passed on to a man called Patrick
Harrison. You have ten seconds to tell me who this man
is, what he is to you, and why you've given him money
from my pocket.'

These days her moods were growing increasingly vol-
atile, and within seconds her temper had risen to match

his own. She faced him furiously. 'To pay Toni's debts,' she said bluntly.

'What do you mean?'

'I thought I could do it discreetly. I never meant you to know anything, but I'm not going to stand for being spoken to like that. Wait here.'

'I'm not going anywhere,' he said ironically as she jumped up from the table.

She was back in a couple of minutes with some papers that she tossed onto the table in front of him. They were the letters that had reached her on the first day of their marriage.

'You knew what Toni was like better than I did,' she said. 'I'm surprised this possibility never occurred to you. He left an avalanche of debts behind him. Not just credit cards. He owed a lot on the car.'

'Surely the insurance covered that?'

'There was something wrong with the insurance. Toni hadn't told the truth on the forms, and that gave them the excuse not to pay up. Patrick was our next-door neighbour. We left him the key. He sent all these on to me, and I sent money to pay them.'

Rinaldo's face was full of chagrin. 'You should have told me.'

'I preferred not to.'

'It was my job to settle his debts.'

'You did settle them,' she pointed out.

Rinaldo threw the papers onto the table and took a ragged breath. 'I apologise for the way I spoke to you.'

'Please don't mention it,' she said sharply. 'In due course Patrick will send me the next statements, showing everything paid, and I'll pass them on to you.'

'There's no need. I accept your word.'

She gave a wry smile. 'You accept my word when I can produce the paperwork to prove it. I wonder if we'll ever see the day when you'll accept my unsupported word?'

He was silent and she thought he didn't mean to answer, but at last he said, 'I was wrong about a good deal. I've admitted that.'

'Very reluctantly.'

'I don't like being wrong.'

'Isn't that a little illogical in our situation?'

'What do you mean?'

'You thought me a devious schemer without a single honest feeling. Would you rather have been right?'

He grimaced. 'If you put it like that, no. You're a disconcerting woman. I never know where you're going to come from next.'

'Maybe I shouldn't have kept all this from you, but—' She made a helpless gesture. 'I suppose you're not the only one with a lot of mistaken pride. I was trying to protect Toni's memory.'

She jumped as his hand slammed down on the table. 'For the love of God, why?' he shouted. 'Why should you protect him? Then or now?'

'Because he needed it,' she cried.

'Was that what you loved about him?' Rinaldo sneered. 'His foolishness? His weakness?'

'Perhaps. I like caring for people, and he needed looking after. He needed *me*. I have to be needed. It's the only way I can live.'

'Is that the kind of man you want, Donna? Not a man at all, but a chick sheltering under your wing? A child in a man's body, clutching your skirts for protection?'

'It's a kind of love.'

He looked at her through narrowed eyes. 'For some women it's the only kind. Must a man be a weakling before you can love him?'

'He must need me before I can love him,' she said fiercely.

'Some men would sooner be dead than have a woman on those terms.'

'Some men know nothing about love,' she flung at him.

The air between them was jagged. This wasn't about Toni. Donna knew she should end the conversation quickly. She could scent danger, not in him for once, but in herself. She'd been unpredictably moody and emotional for the last few days, and now she could feel her control slipping away.

'And my brother knew about love?' Rinaldo asked cynically.

'In a way, yes, he did. He was kind and affectionate, and gentle. I loved his gentleness.'

'You loved his weakness,' Rinaldo said contemptuously.

'What if I did? Doesn't a weak man have the right to be loved too?'

'And how would it have been in a few years? How attractive would his weakness have seemed when you'd grown tired of having to run to me for help whenever he let you down?'

'I would never have run to you for help,' she said flatly.

'You think you wouldn't.'

'Never. And I wouldn't have let him do it either.'

'How would you have stopped him? It was what he'd done all his life. Do you think you would have made all that much difference?'

Something in her snapped and she flung her next words at him, never minding what she said if only she could remove the hateful, cynical look from his face. 'Yes, because he'd have clung to me instead of you. He wouldn't have needed you any more, Rinaldo. That's what you really blame me for, isn't it? The fact that *when he died he was trying to escape you*.'

Before the words were out she knew them to be monstrous, unforgivable. She hadn't meant to be cruel, but he'd lashed her with his own cruelty until she'd lashed back. Now she knew she'd done something terrible. Rinaldo looked like a dead man.

'Get out,' he said softly.

'Rinaldo, please—'

'Get out.'

Horrified, she fled the room.

It was two o'clock in the morning. Donna lay awake, listening for Rinaldo climbing the stairs. For hours now he'd been down there, alone with whatever terrible thoughts she'd left him with.

She blamed herself bitterly for what she'd said. It made no difference that she'd merely responded to his own attack. It was her nature to protect and care, and she knew she'd inflicted another wound on an already injured man.

At last she heard him coming upstairs, moving slowly, as if he had to drag himself under the weight of a crushing burden. She sat up as she realised that his footsteps were coming towards her door. There they stopped. Donna waited in the darkness, her heart beating rapidly.

But then the steps moved away again, and a moment later she heard his door close. She lay still, her thoughts going this way and that, giving her no rest. When she couldn't stand it any longer she got up and threw her dressing gown on.

There was still a light under his door. She tapped gently and after a moment heard him say, 'Come in.'

He was standing by the window, a glass of wine in his hand. A bottle stood nearby, and she realised that he'd drunk a good deal. His eyes glittered when he saw her.

'Come to tell me some more unpleasant truths?' he asked softly.

'No, I came to say I'm sorry. I shouldn't have said that.'

'Why not? It's true, isn't it? He was trying to turn the car so that he wouldn't have to come back and face me. You, on the other hand, were determined to face me, and hurl your victory in my face. You've got courage, I'll admit.'

'Nothing's ever that simple,' she said desperately.

'On the contrary. Some things are exactly that simple. I should have acknowledged it before. You told me the facts weeks ago. Somehow I managed to avoid them— which isn't like me. But you have a way of showing a man the ugly truth about himself—' He drained his glass.

'Rinaldo, please—I don't know the truth about you— any more than you know it about me.'

'The truth is that I'm far more to blame for my brother's death than you are,' he said savagely. 'Let's have it out in the open. I crush everyone I care about because I don't know how to do anything else.'

'I don't believe that,' she said.

'Don't you? It's what you've been saying about me from the start. Why should you have changed your mind?'

She didn't know, except that the sight of him in pain appalled her. It was like seeing a lion brought low, and in spite of everything some part of her wanted him to become himself again: arrogant and domineering, even unlikable. A man who had to be fought. But a man, all the same.

He refilled his glass and sat on the bed. 'Why don't you go away?' he growled.

'Because we can't leave it like this,' she said. 'We're both doing our best in a difficult situation, but it's impossible if we're going to attack each other all the time. We have to call a truce. Can't you see that?'

When he didn't reply she sat down beside him. He looked at her, wary, mistrustful.

'Why did you have to come into our lives at all?' he said slowly. 'Why did he have to fall in love with you?'

'I don't know,' she said helplessly.

He set down his glass and put his hand up, touching her hair, studying her face. *'Why?'* he breathed. 'You're not beautiful—passable, but he dated a hundred women prettier than you. None of them turned our lives upside down as you have.'

He stroked her face, tracing the outline of her cheek, her lips. Donna watched him, unable to tear her eyes away. Rinaldo was in a dangerous mood. His usual steely control had slipped, or rather he'd chosen to let it go. There was no knowing what he'd do now. She knew she should break free quickly, but somehow she couldn't move. His movements, and the strange caressing murmur of his voice, held her transfixed. Her heart was beginning to beat hard, its slow rhythm inducing a sense of drowsiness. All this was happening in a dream.

'What are you?' he whispered. 'Are you human or a cruel spirit sent to torment me? What do you have that makes a man want to—?' He drew a shuddering breath.

Suddenly his hand tightened in her hair, pulling her hard towards him. His other arm came round her shoulders, holding her against his chest while his mouth descended crushingly on hers.

There was no tenderness in his embrace. It was an assertion of authority, of ownership, brooking no refusal. With a movement of alarm she tried to fend him off but he held her tighter while he covered her face with kisses.

'Rinaldo—' she pleaded.

She wasn't sure he heard her. He was murmuring again, looking down into her face with feverish eyes. 'What are you?'

'Just an ordinary woman,' she said hazily. 'Doing her best—floundering a bit—'

'No, you're no ordinary woman. That's just the mask you wear to fool men. Underneath—a devil—a witch— a Madonna—'

She sighed. 'Madonna. Toni said—'

'*Don't speak of Toni!*' he said fiercely. 'Forget him. He's not here. I am. It's my arms that hold you, my mouth that kisses you. Why can't I—?'

He traced his fingers over her cheek, then down to her breasts, now swollen and voluptuous. She knew he must be able to feel the heated pounding beneath.

He drew her close again. This time his kiss was gentler, his lips caressing hers with soft, teasing purpose. The feeling made her sigh. She must stop him—but not yet— it was so sweet. She whispered his name and immediately his arms tightened, pushing her down onto the bed while he kissed her face, her neck, her breasts. The sensation made her wildly ecstatic. She put her hands behind his head, pressing him closer.

'You should have come to me that first night,' he murmured.

'Too late,' she whispered. 'Always—too late—Toni—'

'Toni is dead.'

'Not dead—not while his child—'

Rinaldo stopped as if something had turned him to stone. Donna could feel him become rigid, then begin to shake, as though with a mighty effort.

'Dio mio!' he whispered. 'What am I doing?'

Slowly he released her and drew back. Donna felt herself come out of a dream to find that he was looking at her with horror. She pulled herself up on the bed and moved away. Rinaldo stayed completely still. He seemed transfixed.

Then he moved suddenly, seizing his wineglass and hurling it through the window. They heard it smash on the stone below.

'Go,' he said hoarsely. 'Go, and lock your bedroom door. For both our sakes, *go!*'

CHAPTER SEVEN

THE next morning, when Donna paid her usual visit to Toni's grave, she found Rinaldo there before her. His face was dreadfully pale, and he spoke with an effort.

'I've been waiting for you,' he said. 'Don't worry, I shan't keep you long. I want to apologise for last night, and to assure you that it won't happen again.'

'Rinaldo—'

'Please, just forget everything. You were right about a truce. It's what we have to do, of course.'

He looked ill. There were dark circles under his eyes and his face was taut with strain. But he was in perfect command of himself.

'I'm sure we'll find a way,' she said gently.

He nodded. He suddenly seemed awkward. 'Forget what I said about locking your door. There's no need. I'll never trouble you.' He looked at Toni's grave. 'I'll leave you alone with him now.'

Within a couple of days the money she'd sent to England had been replaced in her bank account. She also had an account at Racci, a gown shop in the Via Condotti in Rome. Donna stared when she saw the address. The years when she'd eagerly read everything she could find about Italy had taught her that this was the most exclusive and expensive street in the city. But when she queried it Rinaldo merely looked surprised.

'My mother had her clothes made there,' he said. 'It's the best.'

'Will you take me?' she asked cautiously.

'No, I'm too busy. Enrico will drive you. He has orders to be at your disposal whenever you wish to go into Rome.'

A few days later Donna was chauffeured to a dark, narrow street in the heart of the city, where most of the shops were so expensive that they didn't bother to display the prices. At one end the road widened suddenly into a piazza out of which climbed a flight of broad steps which looked as if they were covered with flowers. The steps were a gathering point for traders, calmly selling their wares in the shadow of Trinità dei Monti, the huge church at the top that towered over everything.

'The Spanish steps,' she breathed. 'I've always wanted to see them. They're beautiful.'

'They're not really Spanish,' Enrico said with a grin. 'They're Italian, and Trinità dei Monti is French. But that's Italy for you. Nothing is quite the way it seems.'

'Yes,' she murmured. 'I know.'

'Here's Racci,' Enrico said, pulling up outside a small, discreet shop. 'I'll park the car. When you're ready to leave, the shop will send someone to fetch me from the usual place.'

Donna thanked him and got out, wondering about 'the usual place'. Who did Enrico normally bring here? Selina, perhaps? Did Rinaldo pay for her clothes as well as her flat? There was no time to ponder more, for the door was already being pulled open for her.

Inside Racci she was simply taken over. When Donna ventured to suggest that too many expensive clothes would be a waste of money just now, as she was swelling by the day, her protests were waved aside.

'Elegance is of the first importance at all times,' Elisa Racci stated politely but finally. She was a tiny woman in her fifties.

'Of course,' Donna said, trying not to feel intimidated. 'It's just that I don't want to squander my husband's money.'

Signora Racci shrugged. Whether she meant that Rinaldo could afford it, or was simply expressing a general indifference for the problems of husbands, wasn't clear. 'Signor Mantini said that money was no object,' she observed.

Then an assistant produced a draped, olive-green dress that almost made Donna weep with joy. After that she pushed her scruples aside. By the time the session had finished three dresses were being packed up in large boxes and a fitting had been booked for three more that were being specially made.

'Do you want to go straight home?' Enrico asked as he drove her away.

'No, I'd like to see something of Rome first.'

'OK!' Even as he spoke a horn blared at them. Enrico swerved the car expertly and hurled some splendid-sounding Roman curses at various other drivers. 'Your godmother was a cow and your father was a donkey,' he bawled. 'Why don't you put your—?' The rest was lost in more shrieking of horns.

'That's one of the best sights of Rome,' he said cheerfully when it was over. 'Roman drivers. Anything special you want to see?'

It was on the tip of Donna's tongue to say, St Peter's, or the Castel Sant'Angelo, or the Trevi Fountain. But for some reason the words that came out were, 'The Via Veneto.'

Enrico promptly swung the car right, cutting up a goods van, whose driver responded indignantly. After a ritual exchange of pleasantries he said, 'The Via Veneto's a terrific place. Bright lights, exciting people.'

Before long they were in a wide, tree-lined avenue whose shops were as expensive as those in the Via Condotti, but more glittery. There were also luxury hotels and bars, whose tables spilled out onto the broad pavements.

'I'll stop for a coffee,' Donna said.

Enrico glided to a halt beside one of the pavement cafés. 'Shall I return for you in half an hour?' he said.

'Why not have a coffee with me?'

He winked. 'I have a little friend in the next street,' he said conspiratorially.

'In that case,' she said, laughing, 'we'd better make it an hour.'

It was delightful in the shade, and Donna leaned back, enjoying the idyllic setting and the music wafting from the three-piece orchestra, both of which were reflected in the price of the coffee. Three tables away there was a television celebrity whom she'd watched on the screen only the previous night. Women who might have been models strolled past. One especially caught her eye, her figure honed to perfection, her fair hair gleaming in the sun. Then she turned and Donna recognised Selina.

After the first moment there was no surprise. Wasn't this really why she'd come here? She watched as Selina sashayed out of a jewellery shop, carrying the shop's distinctive black and silver bag. Donna wondered what the bag contained, and whose account it had swelled.

Selina approached the kerb, not even glancing at the cars. Donna had already learned that Roman traffic stopped for nobody, whatever the lights might say. But Selina was at ease, almost insolent in the consciousness of her own beauty as she stepped out. Brakes screeched and vehicles came to a sudden halt, curses dying on the drivers' lips as they saw her. They waited with a kind of reverence as Selina crossed in front of them. Then the bedlam resumed.

Selina approached an apartment block and entered the main door. So that was where she dwelt in the flat that was paid for by Donna's husband.

She tried not to dwell on the thought, but her eyes insisted on covering the building. A window opened on the third floor, and behind it she was sure she could make out a flash of blonde hair.

It was a relief when Enrico collected her.

Before long Donna realised that Maria was avoiding her. The old woman seemed to scuttle away if she approached. If she had to talk to Donna she was clearly uneasy, and escaped as soon as possible.

One evening she heard voices coming from Rinaldo's study. The door stood slightly ajar, and she could hear Rinaldo, then Maria. Maria seemed to be weeping, and Donna thought she heard her own name.

She decided that the time had come to take the bull by the horns, and walked inside. Maria was seated on a small sofa, mumbling tearfully, and Rinaldo was beside her in an attitude of comfort.

'I think if I've done something to offend Maria she ought to tell me,' Donna said.

Rinaldo rose and came to her. 'You haven't offended her,' he said. 'She's frightened of you.'

'But why?'

'Because you're a nurse, and Maria is afraid that she has something terribly wrong with her. Her fear has made her avoid doctors, but she thinks you'll know what's the matter, and give her bad news.' He added in a lower voice, 'She has a growth on her hand. Her brother died of an illness that started with a growth, and she's scared out of her wits.'

'Is that why she's been avoiding me?' Donna asked, aghast. 'But—' She checked herself. It was useless asking why Maria didn't seek help. Terror couldn't be reasoned with. Instead she raised her voice and spoke loudly in Italian so that Maria could hear her.

'Maria looks healthy enough to me. Perhaps she's worrying about nothing.'

Tears poured down Maria's face and she shook her head vigorously.

'Well, why don't you let me see?' Donna said firmly. She sat on the sofa and took hold of Maria's hands. The old woman tried to protest. *'Basta!'* Donna said firmly. Enough.

In the face of her calm authority Maria yielded. At once Donna felt the lump on the back of her left hand. Touching it gently, she discovered that it was soft. Maria had given up all resistance, and now hung her head, expecting the worst.

There was a low table near the sofa, with a few books lying on it. Donna laid Maria's hand palm down on the table, took one of the books and put it over the back of the hand. Then, too fast for the others to know what she was doing, she slammed her fist down hard on the book.

Maria screamed with shock rather than pain. Donna calmly removed the book and saw what she had hoped for. The lump had gone.

Maria screamed again and crossed herself, murmuring, *'Santa Maria!'*

'What did you do?' Rinaldo demanded in astonishment, reverting to English.

'It was just fat,' Donna explained. 'I broke it up. It was perfectly harmless.' She put her hands on Maria's shoulders and said gently in Italian, 'But tomorrow we're going to the doctor together, and he'll tell you the same thing.'

'No, no.' Maria was still reluctant, but through her babble of words it became clear that she now regarded it as near sacrilege for anyone to question Donna's word.

'Yes,' Donna said firmly. 'Maria, you call me *patrona*, so treat me as the *patrona* and do as I say. Tomorrow I'm taking you to the doctor.'

'*Sì, signora,*' Maria said meekly.

Later that night Rinaldo asked, 'Are you quite certain of your diagnosis?'

'Almost entirely,' Donna said. 'I'd like a doctor to confirm it, but I'm not expecting any surprises.'

'I'll drive you myself.'

He was as good as his word, arriving home in the middle of the afternoon and escorting them both to the doctor. Maria held Donna's hand tightly all the way, as though there lay her only safety.

As Donna had expected, Dr Marcello, a stout, middle-aged man with a friendly smile, confirmed what she had said, and reproved Maria for not coming earlier. She smiled happily, and looked at Donna with a kind of triumph, as though they shared a secret.

Before going home Rinaldo took them to one of the bars that in Italy sold not only alcohol but also tea, coffee, ice cream and cakes. He bought Maria a huge chocolate sundae. When she'd finished it he promptly bought her another one—'to celebrate'.

His eyes were tender as he regarded the old woman. Now that the weight had been lifted from her shoulders

Maria was like a child released from school. She chattered non-stop, said everything three or four times, and couldn't keep still. Rinaldo listened to her with a loving smile, and showed no impatience, no matter how often Maria repeated herself.

Donna watched him with a kind of aching delight. She hadn't known that this harsh, domineering man could show so much affection and gentleness. But then, he had many different aspects, she realised. Toni had been one man, always the same, whichever way you looked at him. But Rinaldo was many men in one, infinitely fascinating as one vista after another opened up in his character. She listened to him exchanging silly jokes with Maria, and was sad to think that none of this was for her. But perhaps one day...

Then he caught her looking at him, and the laughter faded from his face, leaving only the courteous mask that he normally wore.

But that night before they went to bed he said, 'I must thank you for what you did for Maria. She means a very great deal to me.'

'It was nothing,' Donna said. 'I only wish I'd known before. It's terrible to think of her suffering so much needlessly.'

'Yes, indeed. But it wasn't just your medical skill. You were kind to her.' He paused, and said awkwardly, 'You know how to treat people in distress.'

Seeking a way through to him, she said, 'That was how I met Toni, in hospital. Not that he was in distress. In fact he thought it was all a big joke. You know how he was...' She faltered to a standstill.

'Yes, I remember,' Rinaldo said. 'It's late. You must be tired. Let me escort you to bed. Then I have work to do. And accept my thanks again for your excellent work.'

The brief moment of warmth had gone. The mention of his brother had made him retreat behind a film of ice.

It wasn't in Donna's nature to fret. From then on she concentrated on preparing a nursery for her baby. It led to a clash with Rinaldo, because the room she chose was Toni's. 'It's lovely and sunny,' she explained. 'The perfect place.'

'But it's Toni's room,' Rinaldo said in a hard voice.

'What better place for Toni's child?'

Rinaldo looked about him at the pictures on the wall, the football trophies, the pennants, the little personal knick-knacks. 'You would just sweep all this away?' he demanded.

'Rinaldo, we can't keep Toni alive by making a shrine. Only the dead have shrines. A living baby in here—*Toni's* baby—will make it a place of life again. Can't you see that that's the best way to keep him with us?'

He was silent, brooding.

'Toni will always be alive for us,' Donna persisted. 'He's alive here.' In her fervour she took his hand and placed it over her stomach. For a moment their eyes met and Donna felt something stir in her heart at what she saw. The man was there before her, vulnerable in all his pain and misery. His unhappiness seemed to be one with her own. Now she knew that she could reach him. If only...

The next moment Rinaldo snatched his hand away. 'I'll have his things moved from this room,' he said. 'After that you can do whatever you like with it.'

Within a few hours the contents had vanished and Donna had taken over not only this room but also the one next door, which she meant to make her own. It was smaller than the one she now occupied, but it had a connecting door with the nursery. She wanted to be near her baby at all times.

Rinaldo raised his eyes at the move, but said nothing. He left everything in her hands now.

But he reacted strangely when the olive green dress was delivered from Racci's. His mouth tightened as she lifted it from the box and held it against her. Maria cried out in delight at the perfection of the colour against Donna's warm skin, but Rinaldo left the house without a word.

The mystery was explained that evening when he returned with a small package that he thrust into Donna's hand. Opening it, she gasped at the sight of a ruby necklace.

'You bought this for me?' she said, amazed. 'How lovely! Help me put it on.'

But he didn't come near her. 'It's a gift from Toni,' he said. 'The one he promised you.'

'The one he—?'

'The day you came here, he promised you an olive-green dress. He said the colour would suit you, and he was never wrong about things like that. It's charming that you bought the dress in his honour. In giving you the rubies I'm merely his deputy.'

Now she remembered the conversation she'd had with Toni that first evening, as they'd gone down to dinner. Rinaldo had overheard it. She hadn't bought the dress in Toni's honour. She hadn't even remembered. But Rinaldo had.

'These are really beautiful...' she began.

'They'll suit you, and that's what matters. I should like you to wear them when Selina comes to dinner. She has a gift for the baby that she would like to give you in person. I said you'd call her to settle the date. Here's her number. Now I have some work to do, and I'd prefer not to be disturbed.'

Donna was left turning the rubies over, thinking that she'd never had such a lovely present, given so coldly. She slipped the jewels back into their box, noticing that it came from an address on the Via Veneto, and was black and silver, like the one she'd seen Selina carrying.

She called Selina that evening, and found the other woman all sugar and sympathy.

'*Carissima Donna,*' she purred. 'How are you feeling?'

'Extremely well, thank you.'

'Rinaldo tells me that you've been decorating the nursery, and doing far too much of the work yourself. He keeps saying how worried he is about you.'

Donna didn't miss the significance of that 'keeps saying', with its suggestion of constant contact. And she was shrewd enough to realise that Selina had slipped it in on purpose. She replied brightly, 'No one could ask for a more concerned or attentive husband than Rinaldo. I reassure him that I'm strong and healthy, but you know what he's like.' She gave a conspiratorial chuckle.

'Yes,' Selina said slowly. 'Yes, I do.'

'Anyway, the nursery is finished now,' Donna said. 'I'll look forward to showing it to you when you come to dinner. Shall we say tomorrow night?'

'I simply can't wait,' Selina purred.

If Selina had been more likable Donna would have felt some remorse for having taken her man. As it was, she couldn't make herself feel bad. Selina struck her as a proud, vain, self-absorbed woman, who'd counted on snaring a wealthy husband when her career began to fade. The things she'd said on their wedding day showed that she hadn't given up hope.

Rinaldo's feelings for Selina remained a mystery. If he'd longed to marry her he would surely have done so before now, but he obviously found her a satisfying lover. Why should that have changed now that he was bound in a marriage of duty? He'd saved his brother's woman and his brother's child from lives of hardship, but did duty go further?

And what, after all, did she care if he still shared Selina's bed? Every line of his body bespoke a man of lusty appetites. Once he'd briefly shown that Donna could inspire him with desire, but he hadn't been himself that night, and it had never happened again.

He was to collect Selina in his car, her own having apparently broken down. Donna dressed for the evening with great care. The olive-green silk dress made her look elegant, despite her increasing bump, and the rubies went with it perfectly.

But she knew she might as well not have bothered when Selina walked into the house, attired in a scarlet satin, figure-hugging dress. It had a short skirt that revealed Selina's lovely long legs, her feet adorned with silver sandals. The top was low, revealing a magnificent bosom, and the sheen on the satin emphasised every movement of her curves. Donna, who'd felt reasonably good about herself a moment ago, knew suddenly that she looked like a frump.

The meal was a triumph. Maria had put forth her best efforts to ensure that the new *patrona's* first dinner did her credit. Donna flashed her a smile of gratitude, and began to relax.

As they ate, Selina begged for their advice. 'I don't know what to do,' she said. 'I've been offered another film role. It's a wonderful part, but I'm not sure if I should take it.'

'Why not?' Donna asked.

'Because it means acting with—' She named a notorious B-rank Italian film actor. 'In fact I'm sure he made them offer it to me.'

'Don't touch it,' Rinaldo said at once. 'The man's filth. You know his reputation.'

'But it would be such a wonderful chance for me to get back.'

Her meaning was clear. Having lost Rinaldo, she was trying to revive her career via the casting couch. And she was making sure that he knew about it. Donna resisted the temptation to look at Rinaldo to see how the news affected him, but his arguments showed that he hated the idea.

At last Selina said, 'Ah, well, enough of my problems. I simply must show you my gift.'

She'd brought with her two large suitcases. The first one was full of little garments, all in white. Everything a new-born baby could possibly need was there, several times over. Matinée coats, trousers, mittens, bootees, bonnets, all the best, the most exquisite, the most costly. The centre of the collection was a long christening robe of white satin and lace, with tiny pearl buttons down the front.

To some people this might have seemed enchanting, but Donna felt anger begin to well up inside her. She'd looked forward to buying these things herself, but now there was no need. This tinselly woman, who tried to behave as though she owned Donna's husband, was now acting in a proprietorial way towards her baby.

But none of this could be said. With a huge effort at self-control Donna smiled and said, 'They're beautiful. You—you seem to have thought of everything.'

'I tried to,' Selina cooed. 'Look—' She began to lift the little clothes out of their tissue paper. 'I just know he's going to be the prettiest baby in the world, and he deserves only the best.'

'Or she,' Donna remarked.

'Or she.' Selina's tone admitted the technical possibility, but no more.

Rinaldo had begun taking some of the clothes out, exclaiming over their beauty. The little frown he threw Donna made it clear that he thought she should show more appreciation. Donna pulled herself together and began to say the right things in what she hoped was a suitably enthusiastic voice. But inwardly she was furious.

There was more to come. Selina opened the second case and produced a set of dainty bedclothes, satin-trimmed blankets and soft sheets with embroidered tops. 'I bought these for the nursery,' she said.

'How kind,' Donna said with difficulty. 'After all, I might easily have forgotten.'

Rinaldo scowled at her. Selina's eyes flickered this way and that, seeing everything. 'Do let me go up and see what you've done.'

Before they left the room Selina took a tissue-wrapped object from the second case. It was very large and shapeless, and seriously hampered her as she climbed the stairs. Rinaldo was forced to take her arm and guide her.

'What on earth have you got there?' he asked with a grin.

'Wait and see. It's a surprise. Whoops!'

'Steady,' he said, putting his arm about her waist to help her. Donna walked on ahead, determined to see nothing.

At last Rinaldo threw open the door to the room on which Donna had expended so much love and care. The carpet was a pale biscuit colour, and the walls pale cream with a light green border round the top. Large white cupboards ran along one wall. Donna walked in ahead of the other two, surveying her domain with pardonable pride. Selina exclaimed over everything, but her eyes were cold and shrewd.

'It's beautiful, Donna. Just beautiful,' she said, a wide smile on her face. 'I wonder if—? But of course, you're English. You've created an English nursery, haven't you? And it's charming—charming...' She left the implication hanging in the air.

'I don't think my baby will be troubled about what's English and what's Italian,' Donna said with determined affability, and just the tiniest emphasis on 'my' baby. 'Why don't you show us the big secret in that parcel? We're dying to see it, aren't we, Rinaldo?'

'Of course. Shall I help you open it?'

He assisted Selina to tear off the mountains of wrapping, revealing a huge furry mouse.

'It can sit on the cot, waiting for the baby,' Selina said. 'Let's put him in place.'

Donna stood back as Rinaldo helped her to adjust the mouse. She might have been an onlooker, watching as two proud parents prepared their child's cradle. Somehow Rinaldo and Selina looked right together.

'What shall we call him?' Selina cooed.

'How about Max?' Donna said, trying to be civil.

'Oh, no, that's not a nice name. I know. We'll call him Jojo. Don't you think that suits him, Rinaldo?'

'Anything you like,' he said, grinning.

'Jojo it is, then,' Donna said with a forced smile. 'Thank you, Selina. Excuse me, I think I'll just go and have a word with Maria.'

She stayed away as long as possible, calming her annoyance. When the coffee was ready she carried it in herself. Rinaldo and Selina had returned to the dining room. As she approached the door she could hear Rinaldo talking in an urgent voice.

'You mustn't work with that man. I forbid it.'

'But what else can I do, *caro*? My career is all I have left.'

'Don't say that. I hate to think of you—'

'Here we are,' Donna said, walking into the room with the tray. She smiled at them brightly. 'I'm sorry it took so long.'

CHAPTER EIGHT

DONNA lay awake, counting the minutes in the darkness. It was five hours since Rinaldo had driven Selina home, and still there was no sign of his return. She knew the other woman would have asked him up to her apartment—*their* apartment—and presumably he'd agreed. But what then? Five hours!

Was he with her at this moment, running his hands over that perfect body? A *slim* body, not one thickening with child. Were they using words and caresses whose meaning only they knew?

Donna buried her face into the pillow, trying to shut out the images that tortured her. Her whole body was full of treacherous desire for him. She'd fought it, blaming it on the mood swings of pregnancy. But the memory of his kiss wouldn't be so easily banished. She'd felt as if she was going up in flames. Nothing she'd felt in Toni's arms had equalled that sensation of ecstasy, and now she couldn't forget it. She wanted Rinaldo with every part of her. But he was hers in name only.

Unable to stand it any longer, she rose and put on her dressing gown. The house was silent as she crept downstairs and out into Loretta's garden. She sat by the fountain and scooped up some water to put on her burning brow. It cooled her skin, but it didn't help with the real fever that tortured her.

At last she heard the car draw up outside the house, then his footsteps, coming towards the cloisters. He must have seen the door to the garden standing open, and come to investigate.

'Is anyone there?' His voice came from the darkness. 'Donna?'

He moved towards her, through the moonlit garden. 'What are you doing here at this hour?'

She tried to restrain the words but they burst from her. 'You're late. I thought you'd be home hours ago.'

He looked at her with surprise. 'I thought *you* would have been asleep hours ago. Is it your concern where I go and what I do?'

'I think it is, especially when you're with Selina until the small hours. Everyone knows what she is to you.'

'Indeed.' There was a dangerous note in his voice. 'And just what is she to me?'

'A woman you're keeping,' she flung at him. 'A woman whose rent you pay.'

His mouth twisted. 'I suppose Toni told you that.'

'Is it true?'

'What if it is? If I choose to help out an old friend, that's my business. I won't tolerate your interference in what doesn't concern you. Let that be understood.'

'And I won't tolerate being made a fool of,' she said vehemently. 'You and I know why we made this marriage but the world doesn't. How do you think I'll feel being laughed at because you went straight back to your mistress?'

'My mistress? You take a lot for granted. I've told you, she's an old friend.' There was a steel edge to his voice. 'You'd be well advised to leave it there.'

'And suppose I don't choose to leave it there?' she said angrily.

His voice was soft and dangerous. 'I strongly suggest that you do, Donna.'

'Suggest? Or order?'

'Whichever you like, as long as you do what I say. Don't argue with me, and don't try to dictate to me. A jealous scene is hardly appropriate in our situation.'

'Jealous?' The colour flew to her cheeks, making her glad the darkness hid her. 'How dare you say that? It's nothing to me who you sleep with.'

'Indeed?' he said cruelly. 'No one who'd heard you this last few minutes would have thought so.'

'I told you, I don't like you making a fool of me.'

He regarded her strangely. 'And that's all it is?'

'Of course.'

'So, as long as I'm discreet I can have a mistress with your goodwill. Is that what you're saying? Visit her during the midday siesta, and as long as you don't know there'll be no arguments?'

She gave a shaky laugh. 'I wonder how you'd feel if I took the same attitude.'

The irony vanished from his face to be replaced by thunder. 'That's entirely different.'

'Only for the moment. Once my child is safely born, what's to stop me acting as you do?'

'*I* will stop you. I will not permit it. You'll behave yourself properly as my wife, because I will tolerate nothing else. You'll never so much as look at another man.'

'You're medieval,' she said fiercely. 'You want to be free to do as you please, but keep me in a loveless desert.'

'I *am* free to do as I please. I will not explain myself to you, or account for my actions. As for the desert— why should it come to that? When the child is born we can consider the terms on which our marriage is to be lived.'

'*Your* terms,' she said angrily.

'Of course my terms. This is Italy. I'm not some docile Englishman saying, "Yes, dear," and, "No, dear." I say yes and no as it pleases me.'

She was silent, hating him. But her eyes told of her rebellion, and he stepped closer to her. 'Think what you like of me, Donna,' he said softly. 'But you belong to me. Now and in the future. That's the bargain you've made.'

'Never,' she said furiously. 'Our bargain is a formality. I never agreed to be a piece of property.'

He didn't reply, but she read in his face that a reply was unnecessary. She might rail as much as she pleased. He was master here.

'I think you must be a devil,' she said bitterly.

'No, just an Italian, with an Italian sense of family. A woman from England would hardly understand that, but I told you once, here family counts. You're a Mantini wife, bearing a Mantini child, and you'll behave as a good wife and mother.'

'I'll be a good mother, Rinaldo. You can be sure of that. But you and I aren't husband and wife in any sense that means anything.'

'But we will be, when the time comes. What else were you proposing? To keep to your solitary bed, leaving me to other women? Do you think I'll let you?'

His hands were on her shoulders, drawing her towards him. She made a last-minute effort to struggle free but he had her in a grip of iron, covering her mouth with his own, holding her fast in a crushing embrace.

'Is that the kind of marriage we'll have, Donna?' he whispered against her lips. 'Keeping our distance?'

His mouth was on hers again before she could answer, silencing all protest, kissing her with fierce purpose. 'Do you really think that's how it will be?' he murmured.

'I won't share you,' she said fiercely. 'I won't be a docile Italian wife, turning a blind eye while you do what you please.'

He laughed. 'Then you'll have to find a way to keep me at home, won't you?'

'Stop this,' she begged. 'Let me go. You have no right—'

'You're my wife. You'd be surprised what rights I have. But why should we fight now? Let's save the fight for after the birth—when we might both enjoy it.'

'Let me go.'

'Not yet,' he whispered, bending his head again. 'You belong to me,' he said against her lips. 'Whether you like it or not, you belong to me.'

'No—' She tried to protest but he muffled the words with his mouth. Donna struggled against the violence of her desire, pitting her anger against it. She wanted him but not like this, not on his terms.

'Say it,' he commanded her. 'You belong to me. *Say it*.'

'Never. Not now or ever.'

'Ever is a long time, Donna. Do you think I couldn't make you mine?'

She looked at him steadily, in control of herself again. 'You'll never make me admit it,' she said in a voice that challenged him.

A shadow of anger passed swiftly across his face. 'You have a genius for knowing where to attack, *mia piccola strega*. Of course. Admitting it is everything. Go to bed now. Keep me at a distance while you can, while you can use Toni's child to fend me off. But remember—I'll be waiting.'

* * *

Strangely enough, after that Donna found herself set-
tling into a life of peace and contentment. As she grew
larger her mood swings disappeared and a pleasant calm
pervaded her.

She was popular at the villa. Piero openly adored her,
and the servants had been won over by her care of him,
and what she'd done for Maria. They loved her too for
her constant attendance at Toni's grave, and the attention she showered on Loretta's garden. When Maria
found her there one day, and confided, 'The mistress
would have liked to see you here,' Donna's success with
her household was assured.

She had time to study the garden in detail, and came
to realise that every one of the statues was of Rinaldo
or Toni. Toni was the fat, laughing baby whose hands
constantly reached up to the flowers, and Rinaldo was
the young boy, serious too soon, whose eyes stared ahead
at something that troubled him. Donna wondered if
Loretta had been aware of trouble. Had she understood
her son that well, or had her clever fingers worked it
into the bronze unknowingly?

The man himself behaved punctiliously. He never
again stayed out late with Selina, and if he visited her
at the noon siesta, as he'd half threatened, Donna had
no way of knowing. He was always home on time, his
manner invariably courteous and gentle. But he lived
just apart from her, in a place she couldn't reach.

But this troubled her less now that all her attention
was for her coming baby. Increasingly the household
came to revolve around her. For the first time in her life
she was cocooned by the affection and approval of a
family—a huge family that encompassed everyone in the
Villa Mantini.

She moved into her new room with the connecting door to the nursery. Now she was more than ever aware of Rinaldo's movements, for his room was just across the corridor. She knew when he came to bed, which was usually very late. She knew also that he sometimes paused outside her door. But he never came in.

Their truce held. When he discovered that she loved opera he took her to a performance at the Caracalla Baths, the huge open-air theatre created from the ruins of an ancient Roman sauna. Donna had a vivid imagination and she could picture the building as it had been two thousand years ago, not just a bathhouse but a meeting place for the rulers of the Roman empire.

The programme gave a brief description of Caracalla in its great days, with illustrations. One of them was a profile of a Roman general, fresh from conquering provinces, his hair adorned with laurels. His face was clean-cut, arrogant, full of the certainty of superiority— the classic Roman profile.

Then she glanced sideways at her husband, and saw a profile so similar that she almost gasped. There was the same arrogance and certainty, transmitted down two thousand years. Rinaldo was born of a race of men who'd once subdued the whole world. And the signs were still there. It might be fanciful, but she felt she understood him a little better.

She understood other things too. The Italy she'd dreamed about, the brightly coloured, merry country, full of sun and wine, was only one facet. There was another Italy, a place of dark, fierce passions. They were there in the violent drama on the stage. *Sangue, morte e vendetta*. Blood, death and vengeance. The Italians wrote operas about these things because they were deep in the Italian soul.

But the stormy passions in the music destroyed her calm, and that night she was haunted by a dream that had troubled her recently. She was back in the car. It rocked violently. She fought to keep control of the wheel, but Toni was there, screaming at her that he didn't want to go home. He seized the wheel . . . she tried to fight him off, but he held onto her and her puny strength was useless against the power of the arms about her.

'No,' she screamed. 'Toni, no!'

'Hush now.' The voice was strong and reassuring in her ear. 'Donna, wake up! It's all right.'

She couldn't struggle any more. She collapsed, sobbing helplessly, and felt Rinaldo's arms tighten about her.

'It's all right,' he said. 'It was only a dream. It's over now.'

'No,' she wept. 'It will never be over.'

He switched on the bedside lamp, throwing a mellow glow into the room, then gathered her to him again. Donna leaned against him while tears rolled down her cheeks.

'It was the accident,' she whispered. 'It was happening all over again.'

'I think you have that dream often,' he said.

'Yes. How did you know?'

'I hear you calling in the night. Usually you only cry out once or twice, but tonight it went on and on, and I had to come to you.'

'Sometimes I'm afraid to go to sleep. Toni's there...but when I call him he vanishes, and there's only his grave.'

'You still miss him?' Rinaldo asked heavily.

She was too weak and weary to think of putting on a brave front now. She could only hiccup like a child, and say forlornly, 'He was always kind to me.'

Rinaldo was silent, and she became aware that she was leaning against his bare chest. It was smooth-skinned and muscular, rising and falling with the power of his emotion. He was wearing only pyjama trousers made of silk, and through the thin material she could clearly see the lines of his taut hips and long thighs. A pleasant, warm smell came from his brown skin.

'Yes,' he said at last. 'He was kind. He never thought of tomorrow, any more than a child does. But he laughed and sang and made the house bright with his warmth.'

'I keep half expecting him to come back, and then I won't be so lonely,' Donna said huskily. 'I wait, but he doesn't come, and I feel alone again.'

He pushed her a little away from him and stared down into her face, astonished. 'That's exactly how I feel,' he said in an incredulous voice. 'I look up, thinking I'll see him, laughing in his old merry way. But he's not there, and the empty space is terrible.' He sighed. 'He'll never be here again, for either of us. We both have to live with that.'

He rocked her slowly back and forth. 'There's no need for you to be lonely,' he said. 'You have all of us here to care for you.'

'For the mother of Toni's baby,' she said softly. 'Not for me. Toni cared for *me*; that's why I loved him.'

He looked down at her in surprise. 'That was why?'

'Yes. Just that. I know you thought it was money, but it wasn't. He wanted me so much. No one ever wanted me before.'

Once it would have been impossible to speak this way to Rinaldo, but while he held her so tenderly she suddenly found she could open her heart to him, without fearing his scorn.

'But surely you had a family?' he asked.

'Not really. My father left when I was seven. There was a divorce and he married his other woman. When my mother died I thought he'd take me to live with his new family, but he never did. He made all kinds of excuses, but the fact was that I didn't fit in.'

'Dio mio!' Rinaldo said with soft violence, tightening his arms about her.

'I grew up knowing I didn't belong anywhere. But then there was Toni. He made me feel beautiful, and loved. He talked about his Italian family, and it sounded the most wonderful thing in the world. I dreamed of being part of a real family at last—' She broke off, partly because Rinaldo had brushed his fingers across her mouth.

'Don't,' he whispered. 'I'm to blame. I should have tried to be more understanding.'

'And then I got pregnant and he was thrilled. I thought, Now I've got my family—and then—'

'Hush,' he said fiercely. 'No more. I can't bear it.'

She looked up in wonder at the new note in his voice. His face was haggard. 'It should have been different,' he said. 'Everything was his, and I took it away from him—I killed him—'

'No,' she said swiftly. 'No—that's not true.'

'It is true. We both know it is. It'll always be there. How can we forget?'

'Aagh!' she said suddenly.

'What is it? Is the baby—?'

'No, it's not coming. Just kicking. He's done that a lot recently.'

'He?' Rinaldo asked, with the nearest approach to teasing she'd ever heard from him.

'Got to be a he,' she gasped. 'He's going to be a footballer, from the feel.'

'Can I do something for you?'

'I sometimes make myself some tea during the night—'

'Stay here. I'll go.'

Slightly to her surprise he was back quickly, with a pot of tea that had been properly made.

'This is delicious,' she said, sipping it.

'Can you sleep now?' He saw the wary look that passed over her face. 'What is it? The dream?'

'Yes. Sometimes it comes back.'

'Don't worry. I'll stay with you.' He pressed her gently back against the pillows and pulled the sheet up over her. 'If you seem troubled, I'll wake you.'

'Are you sure?'

'Quite sure. I won't go away. Go to sleep now. I'm here.'

She was already feeling drowsy. It was nice to be able to relax, knowing that she had nothing to fear. He slipped into bed beside her and put his arms about her. Her last conscious thought was of him, solid and reassuring, keeping her safe.

But when she woke in the morning the sun was high in the sky, and Rinaldo had left for work an hour ago.

CHAPTER NINE

As THE year drew on Donna discovered that another of her preconceptions about Italy had been wrong. Although the summer months were scorching hot, winter was just like England, except that possibly the weather was colder. She woke one morning to find Loretta's garden a magical place of frozen beauty, with everything covered by a dusting of sparkling frost. A few days later the snow came, an endless stream of soft white flakes. Icicles hung from the fountains, and everywhere was silent.

The week before Christmas Piero developed a nasty lung infection.

'There's no cause for alarm,' Dr Marcello told them. 'But I'd like to have him back in hospital for a while.'

The day after Piero returned to hospital Rinaldo said, 'We'll visit him tonight, if you feel up to the journey.'

She was eight months pregnant and had recently been feeling tired, but she immediately agreed. By the evening she was beginning to wish she'd said no. Her head was aching and she longed to go to bed early, but she wouldn't disappoint Piero.

Snow had fallen and the air was bitterly cold. She shivered as they left the house, and drew the edges of her coat close.

'Be careful,' Rinaldo said sharply. 'The path is slippery.'

They found Piero in a cheerful mood. The antibiotics were working and his colour had improved. These days

138

his left hand was noticeably stronger and he enjoyed flexing it for their appreciation. He smiled as Donna poured tea for him. But when the smile died his face was full of anxiety. He pointed at Donna, frowning in Rinaldo's direction, then indicated the door.

'I think he wants us to go,' Rinaldo said. Piero gave a grunt of agreement. 'Are you tired, Nonno?'

Piero managed a slight shake of the head and drew a D on the counterpane.

'Donna's tired?' Rinaldo asked, and Piero nodded.

'Are you?' he asked her abruptly.

'A little, yes.'

'Then I'll take you home.'

She kissed Piero, and they left. As they descended the steps she felt Rinaldo's hand under her arm. He never failed in such little gestures of courtesy.

He drove fast, his tense gaze fixed on the road. He was a skilled driver, and despite the treacherous conditions Donna felt no alarm, until he braked sharply and cursed at something he'd seen on the road ahead.

'Traffic jam!' he said. 'I'd forgotten how easily the roads clog at this time of year. It's blocked solid.'

'Oh, no! We could be hours getting home,' she said in despair.

'No, I can take another route.' He wrenched the wheel, turning the car down a side street. 'We'll have to cut across country this way. It's longer but the roads should be free and there'll be less delay.'

Donna couldn't follow the twists they took in the next few minutes, but soon they were out in the country. The lights had disappeared and when she peered out of the window she could only make out fields, stretching into the distance.

'I don't know where we are,' she said. 'Is this anywhere near home?'

'We're almost—*Santa Maria*!' The words were torn from him as the car suddenly skidded on a patch of ice. He fought with the wheel, trying to keep steady, while waves of horror engulfed Donna. She'd lived through this before. The car out of control, the frantic efforts to stabilise it, and the end approaching... She screamed into the darkness.

They stopped with a thunderous impact. Donna sat shivering, trying to grapple with the dread that possessed her mind.

'We've just lurched into the ditch,' Rinaldo said in a shaken voice. 'Are you all right?' Receiving no answer, he looked closely into her face. 'Donna...'

'Over and over...' she whispered. 'Over and over...and he called my name...until there was silence...'

'Donna,' he said firmly, gripping her hands, 'listen to me. It's finished—that other time—we're not turning over. We're just in a ditch. I'm going to get you out and— *Ouch*!' he finished with a small grunt as her nails dug into his hands sharply enough to hurt. She turned to him, wild-eyed.

'The baby,' she gasped. 'It's started.'

'What? It's not due for another month.'

'The shock—'

'My God! I've got to get you back to hospital. All right. Hang on.'

He tried to start the car, but the engine whirred without sparking into life. Donna clutched her stomach, waiting for the next pain, praying that her baby wouldn't be born like this.

Rinaldo got out and placed his shoulder against the front of the car. Donna felt the vehicle rock as he strained to push it out of the ditch. Another pain tore through her. Horrified, she realised that it was only a few minutes since the last. The shock of the impact had sent her into premature labour, and there wasn't much time.

Rinaldo got back in beside her. 'I can't get it free,' he said grimly. 'How are you?'

'Not good. It's coming fast.'

He snatched up the car phone. 'It'll have to be an ambulance, then,' he said, dialling furiously. In a few moments he was talking to the hospital, describing what had happened.

'For God's sake get here quickly,' he said. 'I'll describe where we are.'

But pinpointing exactly where they were in the darkness of the countryside was almost impossible. At last he said, 'Look for a vehicle slewed into the ditch with all the lights on. And try to hurry.' He replaced the phone. 'It may take them half an hour, but babies don't come that fast, surely?'

'Not normally,' Donna said in painful gasps. 'But this is different.' She arched her back. 'If only I could lie down.'

'I can make it flat in the back,' he said.

She heard him thumping seats and pulling levers, then her own seat was eased gently backwards, and he said, 'Slide over. I'll help you.'

Using his hands to steady her, she eased herself sideways and half crawled, half slid until she was lying down in the back of the car. A sharp pain seized her while she was moving and she gasped, biting her lip so as not to cry out. He drew her against him. 'Hold onto me,' he said through gritted teeth.

She did so, digging her nails into his arms until the contraction had passed, and taking deep breaths.

Looking into his eyes, she saw a reflection of her own alarm that the baby might be born like this.

'Is there anything I should do for you?' he asked. 'You'll have to tell me.'

'Give me some support on the left side,' she said. 'The car's sloping a little.'

He retrieved the cushions that he'd pushed aside from the flattened back seats and wedged them in beside her. Before she could thank him another pain tore her apart. She forced back a groan.

'Scream if you want to,' he said desperately. 'With any luck the ambulance driver might hear and find us sooner.'

It made sense but she couldn't force herself to do it. Pride forbade any show of weakness in front of Rinaldo. She gritted her teeth as another pain came. She'd attended births in the past, some of them emergencies, but always in hospital, surrounded by machines to help, and with painkillers available. Nothing had warned her of this terrible raw agony with nothing but her husband's strength to rely on.

She turned to that strength now, burying her face against him as the pain racked her. Somehow she must hang on and help her child to be born safely.

'I'm cold,' she whispered.

Instantly Rinaldo was tearing off his overcoat and laying it over her, tucking it up to the neck. He cradled her in his arms, looking anxiously into her face, but she didn't see him. She'd closed her eyes, trying to gather her energy for the next contraction. The world was dark and full of agony. It seemed impossible that she should survive. A long, mysterious tunnel opened up in her consciousness. Perhaps Toni was waiting for her at the end of it, she thought wildly.

'Rinaldo,' she gasped.

'Yes—yes, I'm here.'

'If—anything happens to me—'

'Hush,' he said quickly.

'But if—if I don't—you won't hate the baby because of me—will you?'

'*Donna*—'

In her pain-crazed state she barely registered that he'd spoken her name—something he rarely did.

'Promise me—'

'Stop talking like that,' he said roughly. 'It's nonsense. You're not going to die.'

The far end of the tunnel was clearer now. She could see him...

'Toni's waiting for me...' she whispered. 'He needs me. He always needed me...'

'And *I* need you. Donna, he isn't there. It's an illusion. Open your eyes. Look at me.' She lay still in his arms, breathing softly. '*Look at me!*' he cried in sudden dread.

At that moment the pain attacked her again with terrible force. She arched against him, reaching up mindlessly to put an arm about his neck. Rinaldo bent his head to her, murmuring words she barely understood.

'It's all right, *carissima*, it's all right—they'll be here soon—'

'No, just you—' she gasped. 'I only want you—'

'I'm here. Hold onto me.'

Their enmity was forgotten now in the space of this greater power that possessed them both. Toni's image vanished. Through the delirium of pain she was conscious only of Rinaldo, holding her close, letting his strength flow into her.

The contractions were coming faster. With terror she realised that the time was only moments away. 'It's coming,' she gasped.

'*Dio mio*! I'll see if there's any sign of the ambulance.'

'No,' she cried, and held him tighter. 'Don't leave me.'

She braced herself against the front seat and felt her baby fight its way into the world. Rinaldo was there to help its journey, and no sooner was it in his hands than he tore off his jacket and wrapped it around the tiny body.

'It's a boy,' he said in wonder. Then his tone changed to one of horror. 'He's not breathing.'

'Give him to me.' Donna held out her arms and took her son into them. She breathed into his mouth, gave him a slight tap on the rump, and the result was all she could have wished. A cry broke from the child, showing that the lungs had started to work.

She felt exhausted, light-headed and triumphant. This was her son, around whom there had been so many storms, born at last, and safe in his mother's arms. He was beautiful.

'Toni,' she whispered. '*Mio piccolo Toni*, after your father.'

Suddenly she was swept by grief for Toni, who'd fathered this beautiful child, and who would never see him. She'd wept before, in sadness for the loss of him, but now her feeling was all for what *he* had lost. He was there in her unsettled mind, smiling as she'd so often seen him, and it seemed intolerable that his smile would never shine on his son. He'd loved life, and passed it on to his child, but his own was silenced for ever beneath a cold marble slab.

Now she could only perceive him dimly at the far end of the tunnel. He wasn't beckoning to her any more, but waving farewell. Sobs choked her as she understood that this had a finality greater even than his death.

Possessed by her grief, she didn't notice Rinaldo watching her closely. He took in everything—the protectiveness of her arms enfolding the baby, the look in her eyes as she gazed down at the little face, the tears on her cheeks. He was waiting for her to look up at him, and include him in the magic circle.

'Donna,' he whispered.

But she couldn't hear. She was saying goodbye to Toni for the last time. 'Toni,' she wept. 'Oh, Toni—Toni—'

Rinaldo listened in silence. Then he turned away and put his hand over his eyes.

There was a flash of light through the car window. Rinaldo came back to life and looked outside, to where the ambulance was just drawing up. Pulling himself together, he climbed out.

After that the medical machine took over. In moments Donna was on a stretcher, being carried to the ambulance, her child held against her breast.

'Are you coming to the hospital with us, *signore*?' the nurse asked.

Rinaldo hesitated. With all his heart he longed to go with his wife and son—no, not his son! Hers and Toni's. She'd called for Toni. Had she been aware of him—Rinaldo—for one moment? She'd cried, 'Don't leave me!' and clung to him. But her eyes had been closed. Who had she really been talking to?

'I'll stay with my car,' he said heavily. 'I must call for help.'

'Very well, *signore*.' The nurse entered the ambulance and slammed the rear door. Rinaldo stood watching as the vehicle's tail-lights vanished into the darkness. Then it was gone and there was only silence and the frozen fields surrounding him. It was hard to believe that just a few moments ago he'd been at one with Donna in the closest experience that could unite a man and woman. At least, that was what he'd thought. But it had been an illusion. He'd helped her bring Toni's child into the world, and now she had no further use for him.

As soon as they reached the hospital baby Toni was whisked away to an incubator.

'But he's going to be all right, isn't he?' Donna pleaded. How often had she reassured mothers in such situations? But this was different. This was her Toni. It was desperately important to make them understand that he was different from all other babies.

But it seemed that they did understand. The nurse spoke to her gently. 'He's going to be fine, but the accident caused him to be born a month early, so we'll take no chances.'

'Will you tell my husband—? Where is he?'

'He stayed with his car.'

'Oh—oh, yes, I see,' she stammered. 'It's an expensive car—I'd forgotten.'

A dark cloud had settled over Donna's heart. In those few dramatic minutes during the birth she'd felt close to him. When the pain had torn through her she'd reached out and he'd been there for her. But the closeness had been an illusion. He'd cared about the child, not about her. Now that Toni's son was born, Rinaldo had no more use for her.

She wished the world would keep still. It was normal to feel weak after giving birth, but this terrible exhaustion was new to her. The nurse's face was swimming and she couldn't see it clearly, but she could make out its sudden look of concern.

*   *   *

While he waited for the garage to send a truck Rinaldo tramped up and down the road. He'd retrieved his overcoat, but his jacket had stayed in the ambulance, protecting the baby, and now it was hard to keep warm. He wished he'd listened to his first instincts and gone with Donna. She neither needed nor wanted him. She'd made that clear. But mightn't that have changed if he'd been with her?

He called the hospital on the car phone, and was alarmed to discover the baby was in an incubator.

'It's a normal precaution when a child is born prematurely,' the nurse reassured him.

'How is my wife?'

For the first time she hesitated. 'Signora Mantini is as well as can be expected in view of what happened.'

'What the devil does that mean?' he asked sharply.

'She began to haemorrhage soon after arriving. Luckily her blood is a common type and we were able to give her an instant transfusion...'

The words swam together. Rinaldo gripped the phone. 'Is her life in danger?'

'There's no need for undue alarm... Hello? Signor Mantini?'

The nurse was talking to empty air. Rinaldo left the keys in the ignition for the mechanic, jumped out of the car and began to run towards the main road. It took him a long time on the icy path, but at last he made it and stood staring into the distance, willing something to come along.

When he finally saw headlights he placed himself in front of the approaching vehicle and waved madly. The driver didn't see him for a long time, but Rinaldo stood his ground. At the last minute the van stopped. The driver leaned out and delivered a stream of highly colourful curses.

'Yes, I know,' Rinaldo said urgently. 'You're right, but I've got to get to the hospital quickly. My wife's just had a baby...'

The driver opened the door at once and cleared some debris off the front seat. The vehicle smelled strongly of garlic, and the driver—a middle-aged man with a heavy moustache and a loud voice—confided that he was a dealer in vegetables. From this he passed on to talking about his wonderful family: his five children, his wife—even his mother-in-law was wonderful.

'Your first?' he demanded.

'First? I—oh, yes, our first child.'

'Our first was born at Christmas too. Wonderful. Like no other Christmas. You'll enjoy it.'

He continued talking like this all the way, cheerfully unaware that he was subjecting his passenger to a form of torture. At the hospital he set him down, demurred at the money Rinaldo pressed into his palm, finally accepted it, and drove away, calling, 'This is the best time of your life.'

Donna was lying with her eyes closed, her face dreadfully pale, her arm attached to a drip. He sat beside her, hurling reproaches at himself. How could he have let her go without him for no other reason than his damnable pride? He fixed his eyes on her face, willing her to wake up as he'd willed the car to come. But this time his will failed. She couldn't hear the silent messages he was sending her. She'd gone somewhere where he was not invited to follow.

Perhaps Toni was there with her, and she didn't want to return to reality. Jealousy, shocking in its violence, possessed him. It was the same feeling that he'd experienced the first night she'd come to the Villa Mantini, when he'd looked at her and known that she was a woman like no other, and that his callow, puppyish young brother had secured her for himself.

His frustrated rage had made him cruel both to her and to Toni. He'd sought any way to prise them apart. Once he thought he'd found the key. For a scorching moment in the garden he'd known that she could be his. She'd known it too. He'd seen it in her eyes. But then she'd snubbed him, accusing him of being willing to seduce his brother's woman.

Her pregnancy had come as a stunning blow. His bitter resentment of the fate that had sent her to him too late had made him lash them both with terrible words. He'd driven them to flight. But for him...

Rinaldo buried his head in his hands, unable to bear his own thoughts.

He rose and walked to the window, trying to break the spell by stretching his limbs. But the spell wouldn't be broken. It carried him remorselessly back to that first evening, when he'd seen her through the spray of the fountain, revelling in the beauty of Loretta's garden, instinctively at home with his mother's artistry. He'd challenged her, and she'd challenged him back, unafraid. So many people were afraid of him, but not her. She belonged at the Villa Mantini. Toni had seen it. Piero had seen it. But to himself the knowledge had brought only torment.

He returned to the bed and knelt down with his lips close to her ear.

'Donna,' he whispered urgently. 'Donna, can you hear me?'

But she lay still and quiet, in a secret world that he could not enter.

CHAPTER TEN

EVERYWHERE was safe and warm: just a soft, comfortable slipping into nothingness.

But Donna couldn't quite take the last step. Someone was preventing her. Someone spoke her name, calling her back to life. Strong fingers clasped her hand, refusing to let her go.

'I need you—Donna, I need you—stay with me—'

She couldn't see his face. There was only the firm clasp of his hands, refusing to be gainsaid, and his voice speaking urgently in her ear. 'I need you—I need you—don't leave me—'

Then she opened her eyes to find that the world had settled back into place. She was in a quiet hospital room, surrounded by machinery, a drip attached to her arm. Standing by the wall was Rinaldo, watching her.

As soon as he saw that she was awake he went to the door and called for the nurse. She came in, smiling.

'That's better. You gave us all a fright.'

'My baby,' she whispered at once.

'Your baby's fine. We put him in an incubator as a precaution, but he didn't need it, and he'll be coming out of it today. We had more worries about you. It took three transfusions to stabilise you.'

'What happened?'

'You started to haemorrhage badly. You lost a lot of blood, and it was quite a struggle to hold onto you.'

Rinaldo came closer to the bed. His eyes were dark and sunken from lack of sleep, but they held an eager expectancy that Donna was too drowsy to notice.

'I feel as if I've been a long way away,' she said.

'You have,' he answered gently. 'You've been in a coma for two days. I thought you weren't coming back.'

'I think I nearly didn't,' she said slowly. 'It was very strange—as though everything was ready for me—and then I couldn't leave. Two days? Have you been here all that time?'

Something that might have been hope died in his eyes, as though a light had gone out, leaving his face as unreadable as before.

'Yes, I've been here,' he said. 'Where else would I be when my wife and son were in danger?'

'Of course—and Toni's really all right? Have you seen him?'

'Several times. He's very well now. The circumstances of his birth don't seem to have troubled him.'

'The circumstances of—? Oh, yes, he was born in the car, wasn't he?' She remembered now that Rinaldo had chosen to stay with his car, rather than come to hospital with her. She wondered how long he'd had to stay there before the recovery van had arrived, but she felt too tired to ask.

A sudden feeling of desolation swept her. This should have been a wonderful moment, one that perhaps might have brought them closer. But the memory of him letting her go to hospital alone had destroyed it. How stupid of her to imagine that the voice and the hands that had drawn her back from death might have belonged to him. Wearily her eyes closed again.

Rinaldo watched her in silence. He felt drained and utterly exhausted. In the two days since he'd ridden to

the hospital in the vegetable van he hadn't closed his
eyes for a moment. He hadn't dared, in case she slipped
away while he wasn't there to hold onto her. He'd stayed
with her, exerting all his force of will to keep her alive,
pleading, praying, *commanding* her to stay with him,
until lack of sleep had made him a little crazy.

He wondered now what it had all been for. She hadn't
known him, and he had a heartbreaking suspicion that
she'd returned against her will. What had she really
wanted during those dark hours when she'd wandered
in the valley of the shadow? To whom had her heart
turned?

One thing he was sure of with increasing bitterness.
It wasn't himself who'd given her the will to live. It was
her love for her baby. He might as well not have been
there.

For Donna the following days were a mixture of joy and
anguish. There was the moment, on Christmas Day,
when her baby was first laid in her arms. Once she'd
dared to hope that it would be Rinaldo who brought
little Toni in and gave him to her, and that they could
share the perfect moment. But he held back while a nurse
gave her the baby, and she was conscious of him watching
her from a distance.

But the next instant all this was forgotten in the feel
of her child nestled close to her. Nothing in her whole
life had been as sweet, or as beautiful. Her arms closed
around him naturally, and he fitted against her breast
as though they were still one.

'Has Piero seen him?' she asked.

'Not yet,' the nurse said.

'Let's take him now.'

They helped her into a wheelchair and settled Toni in her arms. Rinaldo would have kept apart then too, but Donna insisted that he wheel her along the corridor, knowing that the sight would please Piero.

The old man's joy would have been compensation for a thousand griefs. 'This is Toni,' she told him, holding the baby close to him. 'He's come back to us. Happy Christmas.'

Their eyes met in perfect understanding. Rinaldo watched them, saying nothing, and Donna found herself feeling the same sadness for him as she'd felt for his brother, both of them cut off from the joy that filled her life.

She remained in hospital for another fortnight. She could have returned home earlier, but she stayed the extra days to be with Piero, knowing that seeing the baby often did him more good than any medicine. They returned home together on a cold day in January.

Donna spent most of the first few nights in the nursery, watching over her child. When he woke she breast-fed him, and changed him, and when he settled again she sat beside him, watching like a miser gloating over treasure. To her he was pure gold. She couldn't have enough of him. It was a kind of pain to think he was no longer physically a part of her, but the pain vanished when she held him to her breast.

'You're not getting enough sleep yourself,' Rinaldo said one night. He was standing in the doorway watching her as she suckled little Toni, her head bent over him.

She glanced up briefly, but immediately returned her attention to the child, who was concentrating furiously on the task in hand.

'I sleep during the day,' she said. 'With two nurses and Maria fussing about me, what is there for me to do?' She smiled down fondly. 'He really is like Toni, isn't he? What I said to Piero was true. He hasn't really gone away at all.'

She said this to comfort Rinaldo, on whom she knew the loss of his brother weighed heavily. But it didn't seem to please him. Instead, he looked at her awkwardly for a while, before saying, 'There's something I've been meaning to tell you. I have to visit some of the factories that I haven't seen for some time. I should have gone before.'

'Will you be away for long?'

'Perhaps three months. They're in the south, in Calabria. I'll need to spend several weeks in each place. I should be back mid-April.'

Three months without seeing him, she thought. But then Toni gave a little belch, and she laughed with pleasure, revelling in the feel of the little warm body.

'You'll be all right,' Rinaldo said. 'As you say, there are so many people here to look after you—you won't need me.'

But I do need you, she thought. I wanted us to share the first few weeks of Toni's life. It might have brought us closer. Now I know you don't care.

'I'm sure your work is very important,' she said politely. 'Don't hurry back on our account.'

He left the very next morning, and it seemed to Donna that he was glad to be gone. He'd made sure she had the number of his mobile phone.

'There's no point in my giving you the factory numbers because I don't know where I'll be at any one time.' He'd hesitated. 'Take care of yourself,' he'd said gruffly, and had got straight into the car.

At first it was lonely without him, but little Toni absorbed her. There was no chance to feel very lonely while this tiny life depended on her utterly. She breast-fed him whenever possible, occasionally supplementing this with formula.

Everything revolved around the baby. The servants adored him, even the men sneaking away from their work to take 'just a little peep'. Enrico made faces until Toni responded with a small but distinct raspberry, which made him roar with laughter. Maria was never happier than when Donna allowed her to change or bathe the little deity of the household.

Donna could have delegated almost every job to someone else, but she only wanted to hug him to herself. She resisted the temptation, and let everyone have a share in him, but though she smiled and thanked them for their efforts she was always secretly waiting for them to be gone. Then she could take him in her arms and murmur, 'My love—my darling...'

Night was her favourite time, when she could have him all to herself for hours on end, gazing at his tiny sleeping body with silent, passionate adoration.

She talked to Rinaldo most days, sometimes calling him, but mostly waiting for him to make the call. Their talks never lasted long. She described Toni, how he was growing by the day, beginning to smile at her—at least, *she'd* thought it was a smile, though Maria had said it was wind. He responded politely, and they were both relieved when it was time to finish.

The cold of January and February passed away. Rain fell, bringing Loretta's garden back to life for another year. Donna enjoyed standing in the cloisters, watching the showers, with the sun close behind them.

She came in one day to find Maria just putting down the telephone. 'It was the police,' she said. 'They've found Rinaldo's car.'

'You mean he's had an accident?' Donna asked quickly.

'No, not the new one—the one that was stolen.'

'I didn't know he had one stolen,' Donna said blankly. 'Come to think of it, when he left he wasn't driving his usual car, but it didn't really register.'

'The other one was stolen on the night Toni was born,' Maria said.

'But he stayed with it.'

'Not all the time. He called the hospital and they told him you were very ill. So he left the keys in the car for the recovery people, and got a lift from a vegetable van. When he called the recovery firm they said they'd never found the car. Someone must have taken it. Now it's been found, but the police say it's in a bad way.'

Donna hardly heard the last part. Only one thing stood out. 'Rinaldo came to the hospital?'

'You didn't know?'

'I know he was there when I woke up but—he came that same night? In a vegetable van?'

'You think he'd stay away when you were ill? I took him in some clean clothes, and I saw him there. He never left you for a moment, day or night.'

'But why didn't he tell me?' Donna cried.

Maria regarded her with fond exasperation. 'It seems to me,' she said severely, 'that you two never tell each other anything. Best you start, quickly.' She waddled away.

'What do you think of that?' Donna asked Toni as she cuddled him that night. 'It was him all the time, holding onto me. What do you suppose it means?'

Toni gave a little grunt.

'You think he cares about me? So why doesn't he just tell me? Of course, he's a very difficult man. He'll be home soon. And then we'll see...'

Toni didn't answer. He'd fallen asleep.

As exercise and sensible eating returned her figure to normal Donna began to consider a new wardrobe. Signora Racci was eager to help, and Donna spent a satisfying morning in the Via Condotti, being measured.

'I don't think I should order any more,' she said at last, with a touch of guilt.

Elisa Racci appeared to consider the matter judicially. 'Signor Mantini placed no upper limit on your account,' she mused.

Donna chuckled. 'That might be very unwise of him.'

'But of course you wish to celebrate the recovery of your figure. It's understood.'

'In that case, let's see if we can make him wish he'd set an upper limit,' Donna said resolutely.

She wondered at the change that had come over her. At one time she would never have thought of spending so much money on herself, but the birth of her son had given her confidence. In this fertile country, a mother had status, especially if her child was a son. It might be old-fashioned, but it was true. The warmth and approval that surrounded Donna at home had pervaded her with its message, and now she was sure of herself.

Only Rinaldo's return was needed to make that assurance complete. She was a woman who knew where she stood with her child and her household. Soon she would know how she stood with her man.

Her man. She'd called him that instinctively, although he wasn't hers. But in the light of what she'd learned it was easy to believe she could fight for him and win. She gave the shop a mountain of orders, and left wearing a new red dress that had simply demanded to belong to her. Red was one colour she could wear better than Selina.

She'd left Enrico behind today, preferring to travel by taxi. The weather was still cool enough to make walking pleasant, so she went up the Spanish steps, which looked oddly bare before the arrival of the azaleas and the tourists. From here it was no more than a reasonable stroll to the Via Veneto, where she would have coffee before returning home.

She found the little restaurant where she'd been before. Just across the way she could see the apartment block where Selina lived, and she wondered what Selina was doing these days.

A terrible temptation came over her. In her bag were some photographs of Toni—the perfect excuse, if she needed one, for a visit.

Why not drop in on Selina and subtly let her know that war had been declared? She rose and crossed the road to the entrance to the apartments. There was a row of bells with a little label beside each one. Selina lived on the third floor—as Donna thought. She was about to ring the bell when someone came out, and she took the chance to slip in through the open door.

The lift took her to the third floor, and in a moment she was knocking on Selina's door. It was opened by a maid in uniform.

'I'm Signora Mantini,' she said. 'I've called to see Selina. Is she in?'

'No, *signora*. She is away for several weeks.'

'Oh, dear. Do you know where she's gone?'

'She couldn't say exactly, only that she was going south, and might be moving around.'

An uneasy feeling began to creep over Donna at these words, so close an echo of Rinaldo's. 'Do you—know when she'll be back?' she asked.

'Mid-April, she told me.'

'Thank you,' Donna said, hardly knowing what she uttered. She turned blindly and made her way out of the building. Rinaldo and Selina were both absent at the same time, both moving around, both expected back in mid-April. A little mocking voice inside her called her a fool for not having foreseen this. She tried desperately to believe it might be simply a coincidence, but her new-found confidence had run away out of the soles of her feet.

Rinaldo returned home early one evening, without telling anyone he was coming. Unseen, he walked through the house and into Loretta's garden. Donna was there, sitting by the fountain, with the cradle on a bench beside her. She was looking down into the cradle, totally absorbed. Rinaldo couldn't see the baby, but he saw one tiny, starfish hand waving about. Donna chuckled softly and seized it, kissing the fingers one by one. Her face was alight with joy.

He'd seen her with her baby before he left. There had been love in her face, but nothing like this. Then she'd been cautious, always on her guard because he was there. But now she thought herself unobserved, and Rinaldo caught his breath at her look of total, defenceless adoration. Mother and child existed on another plane, where there was only love. There was an ache in his heart that he'd known once before.

He'd been nine when he'd come home from school one day and found his mother cradling his new-born baby brother, looking down into his face with an expression that Rinaldo had thought reserved for himself.

He'd lived all his short life in the knowledge that he was Loretta's darling, superseding even his father in her heart. It had made him feel like a king. In a moment everything had been snatched from him. He was displaced, set aside for the infant whose helplessness could call forth that look of devotion on his mother's face.

It hadn't been exactly like that, of course. Loretta hadn't stopped loving him. She'd gone on listening to him when he wanted to confide, interesting herself in his concerns, and her pride in him had been immense. But he'd had to compete for her time, which had been a shock to a boy who'd believed that the world revolved around him. Suddenly he was no longer first, and it had hurt.

He could still remember how that moment had ended. His mother had glanced up, discovered him watching, and smiled. 'Come and look at little Toni. Isn't he beautiful?' she'd said. And when he'd gone hesitantly towards them she'd laid the baby in his arms.

He could always win her approval by being a good brother, he'd thought. But in time his pretend interest in the baby had turned into the real thing. From the start Toni had possessed charm and a beaming smile that had melted all hearts. Even Rinaldo, serious before his time, couldn't resist it. Often he'd put himself between Toni and trouble, and where Toni was there was usually trouble.

On her death-bed Loretta had whispered, 'Take care of Toni. Protect him...'

This Matter of Marriage

**delivers warmth, humor, romance—
a definite "feel-good" reading experience!**

❧ ❧ ❧

From Hallie McCarthy's Diary:

A new year generally starts out with me writing a few inspiring lines about how I'm going to lose five pounds—let's be honest, it's ten—and pay off all my credit cards, and other high expectations like that. It's the same every January. But *this* year's going to be different.

Oh, I still want to lose those extra pounds, more than ever, but for a different reason.

I want a husband. And eventually a family.

And that means I need a plan. Being a goal-oriented person, I start by identifying what I'm after (MARRIAGE!) and then I work out a logical procedure for getting it. Which, in this case, includes *looking good.* (Not that I look bad now, if I do say so myself. But I'm talking *really* good. Are you listening, thighs?) Because, as I've learned in advertising, *packaging counts.*

So, last week I made *the* decision: *Marriage!*

❧ ❧ ❧

And be sure to look for Debbie's October 1997 title, THREE BRIDES, NO GROOM...three brand-new stories of three friends who discover that Mr. Right has turned into Mr. Wrong...but that doesn't stop them from finding true love—and marriage.

DM497

And he'd said, 'I promise, Mamma.' He'd waited for her to say something for himself, but she'd sighed as if he'd removed her last care, and slipped away.

Rinaldo had loved Toni and he'd tried to protect him, even though at the very last he'd failed. But beneath the brotherly affection there had been a barely acknowledged resentment that the love he'd wanted had always gone to Toni. He'd thought those days were over. Until now.

But this was different. In a moment Donna would notice him. She'd say how much she'd missed him, how glad she was that he'd come back. Anything. But it would be about just the two of them, and would tell him how their marriage was to start.

Then she looked up. For a moment it seemed as though she would make a joyful move towards him, but instead a cloak of reserve seemed to settle over her.

'Come and look at little Toni,' she said. 'Isn't he beautiful?'

CHAPTER ELEVEN

SOMEWHERE in her dreams Donna could hear Toni crying. It went on and on, and she struggled to wake, but the tentacles of sleep clung to her insistently. She was so tired ... but her baby needed her.

At last she managed to open her eyes, and realised that the crying had stopped. For a moment she wondered if it had just been part of a dream, but her instincts told her that Toni had really been calling, and now he was silent.

Then she noticed the door to his room. She'd left it slightly ajar, but now it was closed, and there was a faint sliver of light coming from beneath it.

She moved quietly to the door and listened. From the other side came the sounds of movement, and the faint murmuring of a voice. Donna wondered if she was still dreaming, because the voice sounded like Rinaldo. Softly she nudged the door open.

Rinaldo was there, with Toni, whom he was just laying down on a small table covered with a towel. He held the baby easily, with a hand beneath its head, like a man who was used to babies, and he spoke softly.

'You're surprised to see me, *piccolo bambino*? You thought it would be your *mamma*. But you've worn her out, so we shall let her sleep tonight.'

Donna watched, astounded. In the two weeks since he'd been home Rinaldo had taken no more than a polite interest in the baby. But now he was talking to him as though they instinctively understood the same language.

Toni regarded him intently, his eyes wide and curious. Rinaldo went on speaking in a soft murmur that only just reached her.

'Don't be afraid that I don't know what I'm doing. I've done this before, although not for many years. When my brother was little my mother taught me how to look after him.'

Donna couldn't see Rinaldo's face as he moved around, getting a fresh nappy, but she could hear the smile in his voice as he said, 'I didn't want to do it. I was nine years old. I protested, "Mamma, babies are for girls." But she said, "Every man should know how to look after a baby." And she was right.'

He began to fix the nappy into place on the tiny body, his fingers moving dexterously. 'Is that all right?' he asked at last, speaking seriously, as if sure that Toni could understand him. And perhaps he was right, for Toni gave a small, contented grunt.

'I'll have to get used to these modern nappies,' Rinaldo told him. 'When I last did this, a nappy was a triangle of towelling and you fixed it with a pin. It took practice to become handy with the pin. Once I pricked your fa— my brother, and he yelled the place down.'

Toni made a sound that might almost have been a chuckle. To Donna's incredulous delight Rinaldo grinned. In the soft light from the lamp Donna could just make out the warmth in his eyes as he looked down on the infant. He'd finished now, but instead of returning Toni to bed he gathered him up and sat down with him in his lap. The child lay there contentedly, his tiny arms and legs stuck out in front of him like flippers, his wide eyes fixed on Rinaldo's face.

'Is that better now?' Rinaldo asked. 'You don't mind that it's me? It's time we got to know each other, man to man, and we can't do that when there's a pack of women around.'

Donna gave an involuntary giggle and he looked up quickly, grinning ruefully when he saw her. 'I guess that's it for tonight,' he told Toni. 'Another time.'

He laid him gently back into his cot. 'Do you want to check that I've done everything right?' he asked Donna.

'No, I can see you're a real expert.'

Rinaldo looked around. 'What became of that mouse Selina gave us?'

Donna's face was bland. 'I'm afraid Sasha got it. He's a mouser and no one explained the difference to him.'

He regarded her cynically. 'You didn't happen to shut that cat in here, did you?'

'No, but I gave him the very best fish for supper the next day,' she admitted.

They laughed together. Donna's heart swelled with happiness. Rinaldo switched off the bedside light.

'Thank you,' she said. 'I was a little tired.'

He touched her face. 'Are you tired now?'

Suddenly her heart was racing. 'No,' she whispered. 'Not now.' She reached up and touched his face in return, and his arms slipped around her.

His kiss was gentle, almost tentative. They stood close for a moment, arms about each other, sharing body warmth.

'You smell of baby talc,' she murmured.

'You smell of sleep.'

Nothing was the way she'd feared. Instead of insisting on access to her bed, the way he'd once threatened, he held back until she took his hand.

A few moments later her nightdress fell to the floor, revealing a figure that was still slightly voluptuous. He ran his hands over it with pleasure, caressing her subtly, not demanding but asking. Her flesh responded with a joyful *yes*.

Stripped of the silk pyjamas his own body was lean and hard, enticing her to run her fingers over it. She could feel the steely strength beneath the skin, but it was leashed back now as he slowly incited her to passion.

Of the two, it was she who was the more demanding. Her whole being ached to be one with him. In the four months since the birth she'd regained her health and strength. Her fulfilment as a mother had put a glow in her eyes and a sheen on her skin. Now she was ready to be fulfilled as a woman. It was her right. She loved this man, and tonight she would not be denied.

She gave herself up joyfully to his touch, revelling in the warmth of his body, the hot, masculine odour of his arousal, and the anticipation of love. She was ready for him long before he moved over her, and when he entered her she gave a long, satisfied sigh of completion. It was all so easy. Why had they spent months as strangers when this answered all questions? She gave a soft moan as he thrust slowly deep inside her. She moved her hips in rhythm with his, letting him make the pace now, content only to be in his arms, to be united with him, to be his.

Pain and loneliness melted away. She was doing what she'd been born for, expressing her love for her man. The problems could be dealt with later, but they'd be dealt with more easily because of this perfect experience.

She saw his face, and wondered if she'd imagined his astonished look. Then thoughts faded in the joy of the flesh. She was being carried to heights she'd never dreamed of before, and when the blazing moment was over she found she was drifting down gently into the safety of his arms—and sleep.

She woke to find Rinaldo standing at the window, his body touched by the first light of dawn.

'Come here,' she said blissfully, holding out her hand.

But though he came to her he didn't join her in bed, but stood holding her hand, as if unsure what to do next.

'What's the matter?' she asked, puzzled.

'Nothing—that is—we need to talk, Donna—about many things. I'd meant to talk to you before this—last night took me by surprise.'

'Me too. But does it matter?'

He smiled uneasily. 'Let us talk first,' he said. Stooping, he kissed her lightly and left the room.

What sixth sense warned Selina to call that day? Perhaps it was the instincts of the cat that made her scent danger and pounce while there might still be time.

Donna was in the garden when Maria came to tell her crossly that Selina was in the house and had gone straight to the nursery 'as though she was the mistress here'.

Donna hurried upstairs. In the doorway of the nursery she stopped, her mouth tightening at the sight that met her eyes.

Selina was standing there, with Toni in her arms. She was smiling at the baby in a way that disturbed Donna. There was no fondness in it, only possession and satisfaction. Toni seemed to recognise something wrong, for he was making feeble struggling movements and giving little squeaks of displeasure.

'I'll take him,' Donna said, holding out her arms.

But Selina turned away from her. 'Oh, we're just getting to know each other, aren't we, my little one?'

'I said I'll take him,' Donna repeated.

Selina's grip tightened. 'You really shouldn't be so possessive, Donna. He isn't just your baby, you know.'

'As far as you're concerned he is,' Donna said in a hard voice. 'Give him to me.'

Selina laughed. 'I don't think he wants to go to you. I think he wants to stay with his other *mamma*, don't you, my precious? Yes, of course you do. We've got to get to know each other.'

'Give him to me at once,' Donna said in a voice as quiet as it was deadly.

That got through to Selina at last. Her head shot up and she looked straight into Donna's eyes. What she saw there seemed to decide her, for she shrugged and handed the baby over. Toni relaxed as soon as he was in his mother's arms. She held him against her shoulder, stroking his back and soothing him, and looked at Selina.

'Don't ever speak of yourself as his mother again,' she said.

Selina laughed. '*Dio mio*! You *are* possessive. I know new mothers have strange moods, but this is ridiculous. You ought to get psychiatric help.'

'You're no kind of mother to Toni, and you never will be.'

Selina's green eyes narrowed. 'Well, I wouldn't be too sure of that if I were you.'

'What is that supposed to mean?'

'Oh, really, Donna, hasn't this gone on long enough? Rinaldo only married you to secure his brother's child. It was a sacrifice because he and I were lovers. You knew that, unless you've been too stupid to notice, which wouldn't surprise me.'

Donna's heart was hammering with a kind of fear, but she wouldn't let it show. She faced Selina with her head up and gave back insult for insult.

'I know you've wanted to marry Rinaldo ever since your career began to slide out of sight,' she said. 'It never

was much of a career, was it, Selina? Just bit parts where
you could flaunt your shape. But there are lots of ac-
tresses with nice shapes, and film directors prefer them
in their teens rather than their thirties.'

'I'm twenty-seven,' Selina snapped.

'Of course you are. You've been twenty-seven for the
last five years, haven't you? I don't blame you for trying
to make your assets last, since they're all you've ever
had. But their day has been over for some time now, so
you decided to try to recapture the prize you threw away
thirteen years ago. Do you think Rinaldo hasn't seen
through you all the time? You're fooling yourself.'

Selina's face was dark with rage, but she kept it in
check, and her voice was a smooth purr. 'No, I think
it's you who are fooling yourself, *cara*. Rinaldo and I
understand each other. I came back to him because he
begged me to, and I turned down a dozen parts to do
it. The poor darling was still so desperate for me that
he'd have taken me on any terms.'

'I don't believe you,' Donna said, fighting to keep her
voice steady.

'Don't you know how often he's shared my bed since
he married you? No, I suppose you've buried your head
in the sand. But while you were swelling like a sack
Rinaldo and I were making love anywhere and any time.
Sometimes he came to my apartment, sometimes I
slipped into his office. He has a bedroom there, you
know.

'But we didn't always have each other in bed. Rinaldo
is a man who likes a great deal of sexual variety, but I
don't suppose you've ever had the chance to discover
that. Or have you? Was he kind, just once? I really don't
mind. I told him to do whatever was necessary to keep
you quiet for a while.'

'Rubbish!' Donna said, more confidently than she felt. 'If Rinaldo had wanted to he could have married you before I came on the scene.'

'*Cara*, he begged me to marry him. I was the one who said no. You sneer at my "assets" but I've put in a lot of work on them, and I didn't want them ruined with child-bearing. But you've taken care of that problem for me. As soon as he told me you were pregnant I told him to marry you. He took a little persuading but—'

'Wait a minute,' Donna whispered. 'Are you saying that *you* suggested our marriage? Because I'll never believe that.'

'What difference does it make what you believe? Rinaldo wanted that baby and I showed him the way to get it.'

'Y-you're lying,' Donna stammered.

'Am I? Then where was he in the three months after Toni's birth? Not here looking after you, that's certain.'

'He had business—'

'Business—just then? There was nothing his assistants couldn't handle. You don't even know where he was.'

'He was in Calabria—'

'You telephoned him there, did you?'

'Of course I did—' Donna fell silent as she realised that she'd called him on a mobile phone. He could have been anywhere. Watching her face closely, Selina saw every thought reflected, and her feline smile grew broader.

'In your heart you knew we were together, didn't you? Especially after you called at my flat. We had a wonderful time. After months of your moods and crotchetiness he was ready for a real woman. Desperate in fact.' She laughed out loud. 'Once you even called us when we were actually—'

'That's enough!' Donna screamed.

'Our plan was for him to marry you and divorce you when you'd outlived your usefulness.'

Donna pulled herself together. 'Rinaldo will never divorce me.'

Selina gave a nasty little laugh. 'Why do you think he only married you in a civil ceremony? It makes the divorce so much easier. He's making the arrangements now. You'll be paid off decently, and you'll leave the country and never come back. Toni, of course, will stay here.

'I'm a little surprised that all this comes as a shock to you. I'd have thought Rinaldo would have prepared your mind by now, but he tells me that it's difficult. You're so set in your own way of looking at things that nothing gets through. But truly, hasn't he dropped a hint recently? Never mind. You'll give in at last. You know what he's like when he's determined to have his own way.'

'Get out of my house,' said Donna coldly. 'And never try to set foot in it again.'

Selina raised her eyebrows and a little smile played around her beautiful mouth. 'Oh, yes, of course,' she murmured. 'It's your home, isn't it? For the moment. But soon it will be my home. For years Rinaldo has dreamed of bringing me here. You've just been the lodger.'

Something snapped in Donna. She laid Toni in his cot, then turned back to Selina. The other woman just had time to read the purpose in her eyes, but no time to get out of the way. She put up an arm to defend herself, but Donna reached past it to close her finger and thumb hard on Selina's ear. Selina shrieked.

'You're leaving,' Donna said firmly. She moved out of the room, forcing Selina to go with her. The beautiful

Italian burst into a stream of invective, struggling and trying to free herself.

'Let me go,' she screamed. *'Let me go!'*

'When I'm ready,' Donna said. 'Mind how you go down the stairs.'

Drawn by the noise, servants began to gather in the hall below, witnessing Selina's humiliating descent. Some of them covered their mouths with their hands. Others didn't bother. Two of them pulled open the front doors and actually saluted, grinning. None of them liked Selina.

'Thank you,' Donna said, and marched through, keeping her grip on the writhing woman.

When they reached the car she released her. Selina turned on her. The struggle had disturbed her heavily lacquered hair, which fell forward in stiff chunks, giving her the air of a drunken woman. Her face was red and blotchy and tears poured down her cheeks.

'You'll be sorry for this,' she raged.

'Not nearly as sorry as you'll be if you ever dare come near my husband or my baby again,' Donna informed her.

'*Your* husband—?' Selina began, but stopped as she met Donna's eyes. Something in them made her scramble into the car and start the engine hurriedly.

Donna waited until the vehicle had vanished around a curve in the drive before hurrying back into the house. Her mind was in a turmoil of misery. With all her heart she longed to disbelieve Selina's spiteful accusations, but too many of the details fitted. Rinaldo's absence so soon after Toni's birth, his insistence on giving her only the number of his mobile phone, Selina's disappearance at the same time.

Most ominous of all were his words last night about needing to talk to her. What did he want to say? Had he been, as Selina had said, trying to prepare her mind for an infamous plan?

If there was the slightest chance of that she couldn't risk staying here a moment longer. Even now Selina might be on the phone to him, warning him to get home quickly.

She began to throw clothes into suitcases. She was working from the surface of her mind, refusing to look at the torment that lay below. Despite their unpromising beginning Rinaldo had won her love. Sometimes it had seemed to her that he even wanted it. His unexpected vein of tenderness had delighted her. And all the time he'd been making a fool of her with Selina, his true love. The evidence was all around her, and she'd been a blind fool not to see it.

This was his country, where he had power and she had none. She couldn't risk a battle on his home territory. She had to get back to England before he could stop her.

There was a second car in the garage that she occasionally used. She hurried downstairs with her suitcases and threw them inside. But before leaving she knew there was something she had to do. With Toni in her arms she pushed open the door to Piero's room.

He was alert as soon as he saw her, trying to reach out his hand to her.

'I came to say goodbye,' she said softly. 'I have to go. I'm sorry—I'll miss you—but I *have* to—'

'No—no—' He whispered the words in distress.

It was harder to do this than she'd thought. 'Tell Rinaldo— ' she struggled for words '—tell him—just tell him goodbye.'

She leaned down to press Toni's little face against Piero's. Then she dropped a light kiss on the old man's cheek, and hurried out. His words floated after her. 'No, Donna—don't leave...'

For a couple of hours the house existed in an uneasy limbo. None of the servants knew what to think, except that her departure must be connected with the extraordinary scene with Selina they had witnessed. Everyone was relieved when Rinaldo returned, but relief turned to apprehension when he enquired after the whereabouts of his wife and child.

'You just let her go without knowing where?' he demanded angrily of Maria.

'Don't be angry with me,' Maria said crossly. 'She is the *patrona*. None of us has the right to question her.'

'I thought you liked her,' Rinaldo flung at Maria furiously.

'I do like her,' Maria said. 'And I tell you this: if it weren't for the other thing that happened I'd say she'd gone to escape your nasty temper, and good luck to her. And don't glare at me. I knew you when you were a baby, and I'm not scared of you, even if the others are.'

'What do you mean?' Rinaldo demanded. 'What "other thing that happened"?'

'Selina was here. I don't know what was said between them, but the *patrona* threw her out.'

Rinaldo stared. 'She told her to go?'

'No, she threw her out.'

'You mean—literally?'

'She hauled her down the stairs by her ear,' Maria said with relish. 'Not before time too.'

Before Rinaldo could answer they heard Piero's bell ringing. There was something agitated about the sound. 'I must go to him,' he said quickly.

Upstairs he found Piero sitting up in bed with a look of terrible anxiety on his face. 'It's all right, Nonno. I'm here,' he said, taking the frail hand gently between his own. 'Everything's all right.'

In his heart he had a dread that everything was far from all right, but he hid his alarm.

'Donna...' Piero whispered. '*Donna...*'

'She'll come to see you soon,' Rinaldo said. 'But first we— *Dio mio*! What is that noise?'

The commotion was coming from downstairs. Rinaldo hurried out to the landing and was in time to see Selina reach the foot of the stairs.

'Rinaldo,' she shrieked, seeing him above. 'Oh, thank God you're home.' Her hair and make-up had been repaired, and she presented a beautiful picture as she flew up the stairs and collapsed at his feet in a passion of sobs. Rinaldo seized her arms and hauled her to her feet with an absence of gentleness that should have warned her to be careful.

'What are you hysterical about?' he demanded.

'Donna—she's gone mad—she attacked me—'

'I heard she threw you out. Why, Selina? What did you do?'

'I didn't do anything, I swear it.'

'Have you been playing off your tricks?' he asked. 'Donna wouldn't have gone for you without some reason.'

'I just picked up the baby to cuddle him, because I love him so, and she—she just seemed to go crazy. She's so possessive with that child. She doesn't want to share him with anyone, not even you.'

'She's Toni's mother,' Rinaldo said. 'There's a bond between mother and baby—it's natural.'

'Is it natural for her to be so selfish that she doesn't care how she treats other people?'

'What do you mean?'

'Why do you think she married you?'

Rinaldo gave a grim laugh. 'Because I forced her to.'

'You think you did. After that little show of reluctance she grabbed her chance with both hands. She wanted the family name, for herself and the baby. Now she's got it, all she cares about is getting a divorce and a nice fat settlement.'

'Where did you get these wild ideas?' he snapped.

'She admitted it. She's always known I'm the one person she can't fool. That's why she hates me—because she knows I love you and will fight for you. Today she let the mask slip and I saw the real Donna: selfish, hard and grasping. Why don't you bring her here and make her face me—if she dares?'

'Donna isn't here,' Rinaldo said. 'She left, with Toni.'

Selina's hands flew to her mouth. 'Don't you see? That proves it. Once she'd admitted everything to me she had to go quickly before I warned you.'

'But you didn't warn me,' Rinaldo said coldly. 'You could have telephoned me instead of waiting and giving her a head start.'

'I—I was afraid of her,' Selina said quickly. 'You don't know what she's like—mad, evil—'

'All the more reason for warning me before she took Toni,' Rinaldo said. There was something implacable about his face that Selina couldn't mistake. She gave a little scream.

'Why are we wasting time? If she gets the baby out of the country you'll never see him again.'

Maria had come up the stairs and stood listening to Selina, scowling. Rinaldo swung round to her. 'Did you hear any of this?' he demanded.

'I've told you what I heard,' she retorted. 'There was a fight and the mistress threw her out.' Without favouring either of them with another look, she passed on into Piero's room.

'She attacked me like a madwoman,' Selina protested.

'I doubt that,' Rinaldo said. 'I haven't been married to Donna all these months without learning something about her. And I haven't known you for years, Selina, without knowing how you get your own way. I'm not the gullible boy I used to be. I told you that when I ended our relationship, but you wouldn't listen.'

Selina covered her face with her hands, and when she spoke again it was in trembling, heartbroken tones. 'Think what you like about me. Reject me. Perhaps I've deserved it. All that matters now is little Toni's safety. She's stolen him away from you.'

Aghast, he realised that she was right. Donna had taken Toni and departed without a word to him. However much he distrusted Selina, that was the hard fact he had to face. He felt as if Donna had punched him in the stomach.

He tried to thrust the pain aside, to override it with anger, which was how he'd coped with pain all his life. That had been his magic talisman, his way of coping with all hurt from his mother's death onwards. It had helped him show an indifferent face to the world when his brother had spurned his protection, and had somehow brought him through the horror of Toni's death. Anger was good. It was positive, it conquered weakness, and he dreaded weakness most of all. So now he called on anger to help him again.

At first it was easy. Donna had no right to vanish with the baby. But there were ways of dealing with that.

'Wait for me downstairs,' he said curtly to Selina, and turned to walk away. He was forestalled by Maria, who'd just emerged from Piero's room.

'He wants to talk to you,' she said.

'Not just now. Try to reassure him and say I'll come as soon as possible.' He strode away.

In the bedroom he made a phone call to Gino Forselli, describing Donna's car. 'She's probably driving north to the border,' he said.

'If she only left a couple of hours ago she won't be anywhere near the border yet,' Forselli reassured him. 'I'll put out an alert for her. Do you want her arrested?'

'*No,*' Rinaldo said explosively. 'Just keep her in sight and let me know.'

He slammed down the phone and sat there, shocked to find that the talisman had failed to work. The anger was there, but instead of smothering the pain it made a bitter counterpoint to it. Donna had deceived him, defied him, made a mockery of him. But all that was as nothing beside the fact that she had rejected him.

CHAPTER TWELVE

MARIA appeared in the doorway. 'You must come to Signor Piero now,' she urged. 'It's very important.'

He found Piero sitting up in bed, with a heightened colour and an agitated manner. 'Calm yourself, Nonno,' he said. 'Everything will be all right.'

'No—no—' Piero struggled to speak, but the more agitated he grew, the harder it was for him to form words. He managed to say, 'Donna—' before collapsing back against his pillows.

'What about Donna?' Rinaldo asked.

But Piero could say no more. Looking into his eyes, Rinaldo sensed uneasily that there was something important here, something he was missing.

'What is it?' he asked. 'Try to tell me.'

He felt the old man's left hand move in his own. 'Show me,' he urged.

Using his forefinger, Piero managed to trace a D in Rinaldo's palm.

'Donna?' Piero gave a grunt of agreement. 'What about Donna?'

Piero traced more letters. At first Rinaldo couldn't understand. The letters were clear enough but his mind wouldn't accept them. But Maria, who'd followed him into the room, had no such inhibitions.

'Love,' she said robustly. 'Donna loves you. That's what he's saying.'

'It seems like it, doesn't it?' Rinaldo said bitterly. 'Look, I appreciate what the two of you—'

'*Basta!*' Maria snapped. Rinaldo's head went up in surprise. Maria hadn't spoken to him like that since he was a baby and she his nurse.

'*Basta!*' she repeated. 'When you were young you knew how to listen. Now you're a man you never hear anyone else. Otherwise you'd have heard what your wife has been trying to say all this time. She loves you. I know it. Signor Piero knows it. Even that idiot Enrico knows it. Everyone except you. Because you don't listen.'

And he replied meekly, 'All right, Maria. I'm sorry. But I can't believe it. Why should she run away from me if she loves me? Tell me that.'

'I can't. He can,' Maria said, pointing to Piero.

'What is it, Nonno?'

Slowly Piero traced an S, then an E.

'Selina?' Rinaldo guessed, and Piero grunted. 'What about her?'

This time the letters were traced more strongly, and Rinaldo got the word quickly. 'Lies? Selina tells lies? What lies?'

Slowly it came out. Piero had been close enough to hear everything Selina had said. *Selina. Mistress.*

'Selina my mistress?' Rinaldo said. 'Well, yes, at one time. But that's over. I ended it before my marriage.'

She told Donna no.

'She told Donna that she and I were still—? Are you sure?'

Heard her. Calabria—you and her—she said.

'She told Donna she was with me in Calabria?' Rinaldo said, his eyes narrowing.

True?

'No, of course it's not true,' Rinaldo said explosively.

Piero made more signs in his palm. Rinaldo was on his wavelength now, picking up the ideas before they were fully spelt out.

'She told Donna that our marriage was her idea? That I planned to divorce my wife—marry Selina—and keep the baby?' he asked in a tone of outrage. 'You heard all that?'

Piero managed a faint derisive grin. *Selina stupid. Thinks I can't speak. But—for Donna's sake—*

'Yes, she is stupid,' Rinaldo breathed. 'But I've been even more stupid to be taken in by her. And now my wife is running away because she thinks I'm planning a monstrous trick like that. How could she believe that of me, whatever Selina said?'

'Why should she think well of you?' Maria demanded. 'How have you treated her?'

'I've done my best. It hasn't been easy for either of us.'

Maria made a sound that was perilously like a snort. Rinaldo scowled at her, but she was sharing a smile with Piero and didn't see him. Rinaldo strode out of the room and went searching for Selina.

He found her in Loretta's garden, sitting on the edge of the fountain. She turned to him, with a look of angelic suffering. But it died when she heard his first words.

'You will leave this house and never set foot in it again,' he said bluntly.

Her smile wavered. It was less Rinaldo's words than the expression on his face that made his meaning plain.

'Why—? Rinaldo—'

'Shut up and listen, because this is the last time you and I will ever talk. Two years ago, when you reappeared in my life hinting about the old days, I made it very clear to you that there would never be any question of marriage. I took you into my bed because it suited my pride to get you back on my own terms. I'm not proud of my behaviour now, but I never lied to you.

'I should have finished with you altogether when I married, but you pleaded so convincingly. "Just let us be friends," you said. To save your face, and stop people laughing at you. Like a fool I listened. I even made a parade of our friendship because I was sorry for you. And all the time you've been scheming to turn my wife against me. I know the lies you told her today. Piero heard them and told me.'

'I don't believe you,' she said quickly. 'Why, he can't even get two words out.'

'He found a way, because he loves Donna. I wouldn't have believed such things even of you.'

Selina began to weep beautifully. 'How can you talk to me like this?' She gulped. 'I don't understand.'

'True,' he said ironically. 'You don't understand anything important. You never did. You know nothing about people except in one very narrow sphere. Outside that sphere you're like a blind idiot stumbling through the world. A woman like Donna would be impossible for you to comprehend: her inner beauty, the way she can make everyone love her. And of course love is what you understand less than anything else.'

Selina gave a soft hiss, like a cat. 'Oh, if you're going to say that you love her—'

'My feelings for Donna are something I won't discuss with you,' he said coldly. 'Just talking to you would pollute them. Now leave this house at once. And think yourself lucky I'm not throwing you out the same way my wife did.'

* * *

The little farmhouse was well off the beaten track, and didn't normally accept guests. That was essential, because a hotel would have asked to see Donna's passport. The details would have been recorded and routinely passed on to the police. Then she'd have been apprehended, for Rinaldo was bound to have put out a police alert.

She'd parked the car behind some bushes and approached the farmhouse on foot, her baby in her arms. The farmer and his wife had apparently accepted her story of being stranded. They'd offered her a bed for the night, cooed over little Toni, and fed her a huge meal. She'd had little appetite, but had forced herself to eat to keep her strength up.

She retired to her room early, saw Toni settled, and sat beside him, brooding. She'd pulled the shutters tight, so that no light from her room could be seen outside. She was as safe as she could be in the circumstances, but she wouldn't be easy in her mind until she was back in England.

She knew she ought to try to sleep, but that was impossible. Her mind was full of turmoil. Despite the room's warmth she was shivering. The discovery of her husband's duplicity had shattered her. She'd never really known or understood him, but she'd come to believe he could be trusted. Now she saw that she'd believed it only because she'd wanted to, foolishly letting herself fall in love, and blinding herself to reality.

He was a hard, domineering man who'd go to any lengths to enforce his will, no matter who he had to crush. And he'd never pretended otherwise.

But there were other memories that wouldn't be kept out: moments when he'd shown her unexpected tenderness. Her heart cried out at the thought that they had only been part of a cruel trick to dupe her, but she had to accept it.

Toni woke, and she attended to his needs. He drifted off to sleep again, and she held him close, feeling the sweet warmth of the precious little body. For her baby she would take any risk, face any fear, endure any pain.

But her mind was unruly. It persisted in remembering how Rinaldo loved little Toni, how gently he'd tended him, as loving as any father. He'd lost one Toni, and now he was losing another. It was terrible to do that to him. And yet she had no choice.

When she was sure her baby was asleep she laid him gently back in his travelling cot. 'Goodnight, my darling,' she whispered. 'We'll soon be safe.' Then she leaned her head against the cot and let the tears come. It was the last time she would allow herself the luxury of weeping, but the tears couldn't be denied.

There was a light tap on the door. She dried her eyes and moved across cautiously to open it a crack. What she saw there made her try to slam it shut, but she was too late. Rinaldo had his hand through the gap. Horrified, she backed away and stood between him and Toni.

'You!' she said in a shaking voice. 'Oh, God, I might have known you'd find me.'

Rinaldo shut the door behind him and stood looking at her. His face was strained and his eyes looked sunken, as if with suffering.

'It's a pity you don't know me better than you seem to,' he agreed. 'How could you be taken in by anything Selina said?'

So that was going to be his first approach, she thought wildly. Persuasion, to lure her back into his trap.

'It's no use, Rinaldo,' she said. 'It won't work. I'm not going back, and you can't force me.'

'Have I said I want to force you?'

'It's your way. Force is the thing that works, isn't it?'

'Perhaps in the past,' he said gravely. 'But I know it won't be any use to me now. I want to take you back, but only willingly. If you refuse—'

'I refuse.'

'If you refuse when you hear what I have to say, I'll take you to England myself.'

'No,' she cried. 'That's just another of your tricks. I won't be deceived again.'

He grew pale. 'You really do think I'm a devil, don't you? And perhaps I have only myself to blame. But I swear you can trust me. I only want what will make you happy. Maybe you can be happy with me, but if not—' His face tightened as though the thought gave him pain.

'We can't make each other happy, Rinaldo,' she said. 'Let's end it now, and forget each other.'

'I could never forget you, and I never will,' he said slowly. 'I love you.'

'*No.*' She covered her ears with her hands.

'I can't blame you for not believing me. I've behaved badly because I've been in hell. From the first evening when I saw you in the garden I've known you were the woman nature made for me. I didn't trust you. I didn't even like you. But I wanted you and I'd have done anything to get you. You know how far I was prepared to go that first night, trying to take you away from Toni. And all the time I hated myself for coveting my brother's woman.

'I wasn't just being selfish. I knew you didn't belong with him. It would have been madness for you to marry him. When I learned you were pregnant I wanted to smash things because it meant I'd lost you. I tried to believe the child wasn't his, but I knew the truth in my heart. When he died—' He broke off and closed his eyes.

'We can't forget that,' she cried. 'Whatever else is true, that would always be between us.'

'It mustn't be,' he said fiercely. 'We've come through too much to lose each other now. If you can't love me, say so. But I warn you I won't believe it. Not completely.'

Despite her turmoil she couldn't resist a faint smile at this flash of the old, domineering Rinaldo. 'Of course, you always get your own way, don't you?'

He gave a short, mirthless laugh, mocking himself. 'I thought so. Years ago I determined that in future I'd wrest life to my will, that no woman would ever have it in her power to drive me mad again. But then there was you. I had part of you, but the other part belonged to Toni. In the end I had to face the fact that you really loved him.

'He was always there between us. When the baby was born I thought you'd turn to me, but it was his name you called. I've been wild, crazy with jealousy. I went away because I couldn't stand to watch you looking at the baby and thinking of his father, when it should have been *me*.

'If I could really have got my own way I'd have wiped my brother from your mind. But I couldn't. Nothing I could do—' A shudder possessed him. Donna stood looking at him in wonder, trying to believe what she was hearing. It was impossible, and yet...

'I believe you love me,' he said at last. 'Maybe I only believe it because I want to, because I can't face losing you. And I know you'll never love me as you loved him. I accept that. I'll take—whatever is left. Whatever you feel you can give me. But I have to believe there's *something*.'

It was true. This proud man had humbled himself for her love.

'You fool,' she whispered through her tears. 'There's everything—*everything*—all my heart—all my love.'

He was very pale. 'Don't say it if it isn't true, Donna. Don't say it just to make things right. I'll take you home and make you happy. You can have anything you want. Just be there and love me a little. I can live on crumbs, but I can't live on kindly lies.'

She walked over to him, took his face between her hands and spoke to him very simply. 'You could have had my love long ago—if only you'd wanted it.'

'If I'd *wanted* it! I've always wanted it, but I couldn't get past your love for Toni—' He stopped, for Donna had laid her hand over his mouth.

'That was over long ago. The morning of the accident I'd already decided not to marry him. I'd realised how weak he was, and I knew I couldn't live with it. But when he was dead I forgot the bad things. I could only remember how nice he could be, and I pitied him so much. But you were right. He and I could never have been happy, especially after I met you. I knew you were the one that first night, but I tried not to face it.'

'If only I'd known!' He pulled her into his arms and laid his face against her hair. 'I've been in hell, wanting you, thinking you loved Toni, hating you, hating him, hating myself...'

'I thought you still loved Selina.'

'I haven't loved Selina for thirteen years,' he said emphatically. 'After the lies she told you I never want to see her again. I can't forgive myself for putting you in that position.'

'How do you know what she said?'

'Piero told me. He heard everything. She thought no one could give her away, but I know she told you that our marriage was her idea—that she'd been with me in Calabria—that I planned to get rid of you and marry her. Not a word of it was true. My darling, my love, how could you believe such monstrous stories?'

'But I didn't know what to believe. You forced her on me at every turn.'

Rinaldo groaned. 'I was trying to save her face by staying friends. She begged me to do that. I didn't take her to Calabria. I don't know where she was then. I imagine she vanished for your benefit, so that you'd find her absence suspicious, but she wasn't with me.'

'She made it sound so plausible,' Donna said. 'She said that was why we'd only had a civil ceremony.'

'I wanted to delay the church service until you were really mine. When we make our vows they'll be real vows, not some legal formality in the town hall. The night we made love I dared to hope that you were ready to become my wife in truth. But I'd meant us to talk first.'

He gave a twisted smile. 'It was all planned, everything I was going to say to you. I had some crazy idea that we must talk before we made love, forgetting that love finds its own moment. I wanted you to come to my arms willingly, not just because I'd surprised you.'

'I've always been willing,' she said softly. 'And I always will be.'

He touched her face gently. 'You've been weeping,' he said. 'Love me, and I swear I'll never give you cause to weep again.'

Her mouth was against his before he'd finished speaking. He picked her up and carried her to the bed, lying down with her and holding her against his heart in a gesture of protection.

'Tell me that you belong to me,' he begged, not for the first time.

'Fair exchange?' she murmured. 'Gift for gift?'

'Yes, *I* belong to *you, mi amore.*'

'*Strega?*' she teased.

'No, not witch. How could I ever have called you that? Heart of my heart. Love of my life. Let me hear you say the words.'

'I belong to you,' she whispered, and his kiss silenced all further talk.

There was far more, and better, to come. Their marriage would be full of passion and tenderness, fights, reconciliations, and sometimes even laughter, when she'd taught this too serious man how to laugh. But that was for the years ahead. For now it was enough that they'd found each other.

In his cot Toni stirred, grunted, and went back to sleep.

As Seen on TV!

Free Gift Offer

With a Free Gift proof-of-purchase
from any Harlequin® book, you can receive
a beautiful cubic zirconia pendant.

This stunning marquise-shaped stone is a genuine cubic
zirconia—accented by an 18" gold tone necklace.
(Approximate retail value $19.95)

Send for yours today...
compliments of ❧ HARLEQUIN®

To receive your free gift, a cubic zirconia pendant, send us one original proof-of-
purchase, photocopies not accepted, from the back of any Harlequin Romance®,
Harlequin Presents®, Harlequin Temptation®, Harlequin Superromance®, Harlequin
Intrigue®, Harlequin American Romance®, or Harlequin Historicals® title available in
February, March or April at your favorite retail outlet, together with the Free Gift
Certificate, plus a check or money order for $1.65 U.S./$2.15 CAN. (do not send cash) to
cover postage and handling, payable to Harlequin Free Gift Offer. We will send you the
specified gift. Allow 6 to 8 weeks for delivery. Offer good until April 30, 1997, or while
quantities last. Offer valid in the U.S. and Canada only.

Free Gift Certificate

Name: _____

Address: _____

City: _____ State/Province: _____ Zip/Postal Code: _____

Mail this certificate, one proof-of-purchase and a check or money order for postage
and handling to: HARLEQUIN FREE GIFT OFFER 1997. In the U.S.: 3010 Walden
Avenue, P.O. Box 9071, Buffalo NY 14269-9057. In Canada: P.O. Box 604, Fort Erie,
Ontario L2Z 5X3.

FREE GIFT OFFER
ONE PROOF-OF-PURCHASE
To collect your fabulous FREE GIFT, a cubic zirconia pendant, you must include this
original proof-of-purchase for each gift with the properly completed Free Gift Certificate.

084-KEZ

084-KEZ

Take 4 bestselling love stories FREE

Plus get a FREE surprise gift!

Special Limited-time Offer

Mail to Harlequin Reader Service®

P.O. Box 609
Fort Erie, Ontario
L2A 5X3

YES! Please send me 4 free Harlequin Romance® novels and my free surprise gift. Then send me 6 brand-new novels every month, which I will receive months before they appear in bookstores. Bill me at the low price of $3.10 each plus 25¢ delivery and GST*. That's the complete price and a savings of over 10% off the cover prices—quite a bargain! I understand that accepting the books and gift places me under no obligation ever to buy any books. I can always return a shipment and cancel at any time. Even if I never buy another book from Harlequin, the 4 free books and the surprise gift are mine to keep forever.

316 BPA A3UC

Name	(PLEASE PRINT)	
Address	Apt. No.	
City	Province	Postal Code

This offer is limited to one order per household and not valid to present Harlequin Romance® subscribers. *Terms and prices are subject to change without notice. Canadian residents will be charged applicable provincial taxes and GST.

CROM-696   ©1990 Harlequin Enterprises Limited

Happy
Birthday to

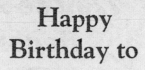

It's party time....
This year is our
40th anniversary!

**Forty years of
bringing you the best
in romance fiction—and
the best just keeps
getting better!**

To celebrate, we're planning
three months of fun, and prizes.

Not to mention, of course,
some fabulous books...

The party starts in **April** with:

Betty Neels
Emma Richmond
Kate Denton
Barbara McMahon

Come join the party!

You're About to Become a Privileged Woman

Reap the rewards of fabulous free gifts and benefits with proofs-of-purchase from Harlequin and Silhouette books

Pages & Privileges™

It's our way of thanking you for buying our books at your favorite retail stores.

PROOF OF PURCHASE

HR-PP23

Offer expires March 31, 1997

Pages & Privileges ™

Harlequin and Silhouette—
the most privileged readers in the world!

For more information about Harlequin and Silhouette's PAGES & PRIVILEGES program call the Pages & Privileges Benefits Desk: 1-503-794-2499

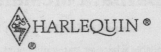

HARLEQUIN ®

HR-PP23